THE STONES

JANET HICKMAN

THE STONES

ILLUSTRATED BY RICHARD CUFFARI

MACMILLAN PUBLISHING CO., INC.
New York
COLLIER MACMILLAN PUBLISHERS
London

Macmillan Publishing Co., Inc.
866 Third Avenue, New York, N.Y. 10022
Collier Macmillan Canada, Ltd.

Printed in the United States of America

10 9 8 7 6 5 4 3 2

LIBRARY OF CONGRESS CATALOGING IN PUBLICATION DATA

Hickman, Janet.
    The stones.
    SUMMARY: While his father is fighting in Europe, a young American boy, motivated by misguided patriotism, harasses an old man who has a German name.
    [1. World War, 1939–1945—Fiction] I. Cuffari, Richard, date II. Title.
PZ7.H5314St   [Fic]   76–11037
ISBN 0–02–743760–4

FOR WOODY AND HOLLY

THE STONES

CHAPTER 1

Garrett woke slowly, opening one eye and then the other. He glanced at Linnie's cut-down crib and saw that she was still asleep, her arm tight around Stuffed Mabel's calico legs. For that he was thankful. His little sister usually got up with a cross face on, whining. *Garrett, tie my shoes. Garrett, button me. Garrett, play with me. If you don't, I'll go tell.* Maybe she'd sleep till noon.

Between his bed and the crib was a nightstand with treasures in the drawer: two magazines about flying; the works of an alarm clock, carefully taken apart and labeled; a collection of flashlight batteries, mostly worn out; a packet of letters reread so often that the edges had begun to tear. On top, the stand was bare except for one handsomely framed photograph. Garrett studied the picture intently. "Good morning, Dad," he whispered.

His father's face grinned from behind the glass, eyes twinkling below his military cap. His father's nose was wider than his own, his father's cheeks were fuller, his father's hair was lighter. But I do look like him, Garrett thought. I look like the pictures of him when he was a boy. Garrett's insides twisted up as if they'd been wound with a rubber band. Why couldn't the war be over? Why couldn't Hitler and the ugly old Germans just quit running all over everybody and let his dad come home? Garrett swallowed and eventually the bad moment passed, as it did each morning.

"Good morning," he whispered again, sitting up. "Listen, Sergeant McKay, sir, I'd like to report that we've got a beautiful day here. I sure wish you were at home so we could—"

"Garrett?" Linnie's voice came wobbling out of her rumpled covers. "Who you talking to?"

"Nobody!" He slammed his feet against the floor and reached for his jeans.

"You were too!" Linnie sat up with the sheet tangled around her and a crease in one cheek from sleeping on a wrinkle. "Stuffed Mabel heard you."

"Stuffed Mabel has stuffed ears," said Garrett irritably. "She didn't hear one word." Of all things, he didn't want Linnie to know that he talked to the picture. She would laugh. Or worse, she might tell someone. She wouldn't understand, that was sure. Linnie didn't even remember their father, or so she claimed. Granpop said that was reasonable, since Linnie had been on the baby side of three when their father was home on leave the last time. And that had been more than a year ago—forever, almost. Garrett thought she did remember, a little bit at least, and only pretended not to. Linnie was contrary; even Aunt Em said so.

The little girl cradled her rag doll under her chin. "You made Stuffed Mabel cry," she said. Linnie began to wail, her mouth hidden in Mabel's orange yarn hair.

"Cut it out," Garrett commanded. "You sound like Fishers' coon dog." He had only just realized how late it was. Already the sun lay spread across the brown-painted floor like warm butter on a pancake. Mom would be gone to work by now, to the shoe factory in Springtown where his father had worked before. Aunt Em would be downstairs waiting to make him eat more than he wanted for breakfast, and then Granpop might need his help in the barn or in the huge garden that they kept in Aunt Em's side lot. He'd never get away. Automatically he patted the bulging pockets of his jeans. He had to hurry.

At ten o'clock, in the lane behind Jack Tramp's place, the Chiefs of Staff were meeting to plan the afternoon battle. He reached into his left pocket, checking. The load seemed to be all right—hard green apples saved from the beginning of summer, no bigger than marbles and just as hard. Stanley Middleton had promised he could be in charge of munitions if he'd bring them.

Garrett struggled with his shirt and his shoes, ignoring Linnie's babble. "Stuffed Mabel is going to visit her grandmother today and have some pickled pears. Pickled pears is Stuffed Mabel's favorite. Once she got a belly ache from . . . ."He went past his parents' empty bedroom and down the stairs two steps at a time. If he could get through the corner of the kitchen and out the screen door without its squeaking, he'd be free.

"No need to try sneaking off," said a sharp voice. Aunt Em was at the stove, her back to him, and she spoke without turning around. She was short and thin as a stick, with knees and elbows that made Garrett think of the rough little knobs on a maple twig. Her gray hair was braided and pulled tight into a wreath that circled her head, but wisps of curl had escaped to dance over her forehead and around her ears while she worked.

"Mush and molasses," she announced. "Wash your hands

and sit down. If you ever expect to get as big as Andy, you've got to eat."

Garrett sighed and did as he was told. Except for Linnie, no one disagreed with his great-aunt Emma McKay, at least not right to her face. She was Granpop's elder sister, who lived across from the old orchard in a well-scrubbed house of her own. But she had always spent so much of her time in this kitchen that Garrett thought of her as part of it, just like the square black clock on the shelf and the green wicker rocking chair. For years, long before Garrett's time, Aunt Em had looked after Granpop and Andy, Garrett's father. Granpop's wife—Garrett's grandma—had died when she was just a young woman. Garrett had counted the snapshots in the family album, and there were only four of Grandma, but thirty-seven of Aunt Em.

Now Aunt Em looked after Granpop and Garrett and Linnie while Mom worked at the shoe factory. Mom worked because of the war, so it was all right, though sometimes Garrett wished she could be home for breakfast time at least. Mom let him eat cornflakes. Aunt Em didn't believe in children eating cornflakes for breakfast, though she never said a word to Granpop when *he* did it.

"Eat!" directed Aunt Em, handing Garrett a full plate. She had a firm mind about everything, most particularly about what children should be fed and how much of it, and when. Eating right gave you spunk, Aunt Em was fond of saying. Spirit. Get-up-and-go. Garrett could tell that Aunt Em had eaten right her whole life long, because she had plenty of spunk, and that was the truth.

Once a tramp had come by at the back door asking for something to eat, and Aunt Em had given him fried potatoes and sausage. It was a monstrous big plateful, Garrett remembered, and halfway through it the man had stopped and belched. "A mite too much grease for my digestion," he had said, pushing away the plate. Aunt Em got red in the face and picked up the broom. "What say?" she had demanded. "My hearing's a bit touchy." Which it wasn't. But the man repeated himself, and she nodded grimly. "Thought that's what you said." She lifted the broom and gave him two whacks before he could get out the door. Afterward, when she was all calmed down, she had laughed until she cried. "Did you ever see the like of his face? I put him on the road, didn't I? I'd reckon!" Garrett remembered that time with admiration and did his best to eat what was put before him.

"Don't gulp," said Aunt Em, settling across the table from him. She had a cup of tea and yesterday's newspaper. "No need to hurry," she said. "Leo's got things all done out to the barn by now, and he said you could let the garden go till tomorrow."

Good old Granpop, thought Garrett, grinning for the first time that morning. He imagined himself already on the way to Jack Tramp's lane, on the way to his meeting with Stanley Middleton and the Grant brothers—Clarence and Beanie—and David Ray Allen. The only bad thing was, they were all older than Garrett and they didn't let him forget it. When school started in the fall, even David Ray and Beanie would be going upstairs with the junior high, but Garrett would still be in Mrs. Anderson's fifth and sixth grade room. Grateful as he was that they let him be part of the gang at all, he still hated being last at everything and the automatic target of all their jokes. He wished his father would come home and tell him what to do about it.

Once Garrett had tried to talk it out with Granpop. They had been in the barn at chore time with everything quiet, and the cats rubbing Garrett's ankles in anticipation of the warm milk he would put in their pan. "It isn't fair," he had said. "We'll be playing ball or something and first thing you know Clarence gets on his bike and takes off and they all go right along after and don't even ask me. And David Ray's the only one who ever even says 'See ya' or anything like that. When Dad comes home it won't be that way, I bet." Granpop went on milking, in that patient way he had, maddeningly slow. "Won't make any difference," he said at last. "It's you for it."

What did that mean, anyway? Garrett wondered, thinking back. When his Dad got home everything in the whole world would be better than it was now. His Dad would probably get him a bike, for one thing, and teach him to wrestle so that he could build up his muscles. . . . He thought about it so hard that he quit eating, with the mush not yet half gone.

But Aunt Em didn't notice his plate. She was bent over page six of the *Springtown Leader*, looking at a column of fine print. All at once she hooted. "Look at this! Old Jack got his name in the paper. Delinquent taxes. See?" She thrust the paper toward Garrett. "If you don't pay your taxes on time they put your name in the paper. Poor old fool. Bet he hasn't got a dime. That's what happens to a painter that gets too old to climb a ladder and balance his bucket at the same time. Everything he ever did earn got burned up in fancy cigar smoke, I'll wager that." She rubbed her nose vigorously in memory of the strength of Jack Tramp's cigars. "He'll end up at the County Farm yet, you mark my words."

Garrett squinted at the newspaper. "I don't see any Jack Tramp—" He ran his finger down the list, leaving a sticky smudge of molasses.

Aunt Em scowled and wiped at it with her thumb, which made a bigger smudge. She scowled again. "They don't use nicknames on the tax books, child."

"Oh." Garrett tried to remember Jack Tramp's given name, but he couldn't. "I never even think about him having any other name but that. Everyone calls him Jack."

"It's Schilling," said Aunt Em. "Adolf Schilling. See right there?" She tapped the paper just to the right of the smudge.

"Adolf!" Garrett's eyes popped like marbles. "Just like Adolf Hitler!"

Aunt Em gave him a look. "What a thing to think of." She drew the paper back, turned to a new page, and drank her tea.

Garrett jiggled in his chair. He couldn't wait to tell David Ray and the others. It was an absolutely perfect thing to have discovered. He might even get to be Chief Intelligence Officer because of it.

"See you later, Aunt Em," he said, sloshing the last of the milk out of his cup.

"No, you won't." She smacked the paper down on the table and got up. "You'll see me now. You aren't going anywhere this morning, boy. I need you to look after Linnie, if she ever gets down here. She can't be underfoot while I can the tomatoes. And land, there's tomatoes from here to next year. Leo might have to put up another shelf in the cellar to hold them all. Now where'd I put that knife?"

Aunt Em began to talk to herself, mumbling about her

best paring knife, and Garrett clenched up his toes inside his shoes so that he wouldn't feel like kicking the chair. "*Okay!*" he said finally. "I'll take her with me."

"Uhh—" It was hard to tell whether Aunt Em had answered him or found her knife. "Where'll you be?"

"Around."

"Who with?"

Garrett considered. "David Ray Allen," he said. "Probably."

Aunt Em liked David Ray, who had carrot-colored hair and a talent for doing outlandish things. He could make her laugh.

Aunt Em began peeling a tomato. "Who else?"

Garrett fidgeted. "Stanley, maybe."

"I thought as much. And Clarence Grant, likely, and that brother of his that trampled all over my tulip bed last spring." Tomato juice ran along Aunt Em's wrist and arm, and she shook it off. "You stay away from that bunch. Whatever they're up to, I don't want you in it—you hear?"

"I hear." What he heard, with the secret ear of imagination, was Stanley Middleton scoffing: *McKay's a dumb little kid. Why do we wait around for him, anyway?*

What Linnie wanted, when her own breakfast was finally done, was to be taken for a walk. Or Stuffed Mabel did.

"Mabel has to go see her grandma," announced Linnie.

The day was already hot, all outdoors green and steamy. Garrett took advantage of the shade: first the willow by the house, then the maples along the pasture fence. On the road, though, there was no escaping the sun. He whistled and walked faster, but Linnie hung back.

"Where we going?" she demanded, standing on one foot and then the other to keep her toes off the pavement.

"To see Stuffed Mabel's grandmother. Hurry up!" Garrett bit the tip of his tongue, hoping she'd come along without a fuss.

Linnie's chin jutted out, and her lower lip rolled forward in a pout. She looked back at Granpop's house with the pasture on one side and the orchard on the other. Beyond the backyard was a shed and a chicken coop and then a barn lot, where the old gray barn and slatted corncrib leaned against one another in mutual support. Behind the barn at the foot of a gentle slope lay a cornfield, and at the far end of the cornfield was a line of trees that marked the bank of Elm Creek. Off to the right, just where the creek

curved out of sight, was a mountainous stack of gray stones, partly hidden among the trees. The Stones were all that remained of an unfinished railway bridge begun and abandoned so long ago that not even Granpop could remember it. Linnie's eyes rested on the place, and she smiled.

"We're going the wrong way," she said. "Stuffed Mabel's grandma lives at the Stones."

"Aw, Linnie, forget it. I can't take you way down there. C'mon." He started off again, hurrying across the road. There might still be time.

"Why can't we?" cried Linnie, not following.

"Because Aunt Em would skin me like a banana, that's why. I can't swim, you can't swim—you know how she goes on about it. Now come *on*, will you?"

"No." She squatted down at the roadside, glaring at him, and began to wind the fingers of her right hand into one of her long brown curls.

He tried coaxing. "We'll take a nice walk, Linnie. Come on. It'll be shady. We'll just go across the road up Jack's lane and around the bend, and pretty soon we'll come back. Okay?"

"No."

"Why not? Will you tell me that, huh?" He rubbed the hard, lumpy apples in his pocket, wishing he could just leave her sitting there with her bad temper for company. He couldn't, of course. One of the things his father had told him to do was to help look after Linnie. Rosebud, Dad had called her, because of the bright pink spots that came on each cheek when she played too hard, or when she cried. "Take care of Rosebud for me, will you, pal?" Remembering, Garrett frowned. Dad should see his Rosebud now, with her thorns sticking out. He went back to her and crouched down.

"What's wrong with taking a little walk up the lane?"

Linnie let her head droop down, and she took a sudden interest in fluffing up Stuffed Mabel's petticoat. "I'm afraid," she said. "Jack Tramp might see me."

"So what?"

"He might catch me." She looked up, and her eyes were huge and fearful. "And then he'd lock me up in his garage and give me to the salvage man when he comes and I'd never see Mom any more."

Garrett couldn't stop himself—he laughed. "Where'd you hear a wild story like that?" he asked her.

"It's true, Garrett! David Ray said so. One day he told me never ever to come to the lane. That's what would happen. He said so."

Garrett shook his head slowly. He was filled with silent regard for David Ray, who thought of everything. The war game was to be a secret, even from Linnie. It was only right, he had to admit. Jack Tramp's property was German territory, his house was Berlin, his old frame toilet was a V-2 rocket factory, and his garage a concentration camp. If Linnie heard about any of that, she'd be sure to talk about it and spoil everything. He supposed he ought to tell her not to worry, though. Granpop said Jack was harmless, for all his loud talk and odd ways. Unpredictable, but harmless.

"He's probably not even home, Linnie," was what Garrett finally said. "Look over there and see." Jack Tramp's house was a single-room affair, with one door and two windows. The paint had long since peeled, the doorstoop sagged, and a bin of salvage paper overflowed onto the steps. "Look how everything's all closed up," Garrett said. "If he's in there he's roasting like a turkey."

Linnie didn't smile. "Probably he's hiding. Behind the water barrel or somewhere. Or out in the bean rows."

Garrett grinned. "He wouldn't hide in his garden, for pete's sake. You know how he is about his garden." Jack Tramp fussed over each growing leaf the way Preacher Martin said God watched the sparrows. And Jack's yard showed the same painstaking attention; he kept it trimmed close as a Marine's haircut. The garden and the yard were so remarkably neat that the house and rickety garage looked all the worse in comparison.

Linnie peeked around Stuffed Mabel and despite the August heat, she shivered. "I bet he's there somewhere."

Garrett sighed and tossed away one of his green apples in disgust. "Well, come on, then," he said. "If you don't want to go by Jack's, we won't. We'll go see if there's a letter."

Linnie scrambled to her feet. "Stuffed Mabel just loves the Post Office," she said.

There might be a letter from Dad, Garrett thought, and that would make up for missing the boys. He began to whistle as he led the way along the road past the garden and the orchard and Aunt Em's house, past Mrs. Tanner's, past the Gillespies'. By the time they came to Fiddler's Auto Garage he was sweating. The garage was one of Garrett's favorite places, with its inviting odors of gasoline and hot grease and its side lot full of broken-down tractors. He would have liked to stop and go inside to see whose truck was on the rack and to listen to the men tell stories. But Linnie wrinkled up her nose and walked faster.

Four more houses, and then the crossroads. From there

it was possible to turn around slowly and see all the town had to offer: Cook's Store, the schoolyard, the cemetery, the township hall, Preacher Martin's church, and the Post Office with MERRITTSBURG lettered on the window. From the crossroads it was also possible to see the house where David Ray Allen lived, and Garrett strained to see whether his friend's bicycle was in its regular place in the bushes by the porch. Much as Garrett looked, he couldn't tell. There wasn't a boy in sight, except for Arnold Anderson, who was only six and not of much use for anything. Jack Tramp's real name stayed on the back of Garrett's tongue waiting to be said, itchy as a cough in church.

He thought about mentioning it to Paul Darcy in the Post Office, but Mr. Darcy didn't give him a chance.

"Good morning, good morning!" boomed the postmaster, and his huge stomach shook. Linnie stared so hard at the great blue curve of his shirt that Garrett had to poke her.

"Peppermint for the ladies!" Mr. Darcy inclined his bald head across the counter to Linnie, eyes twinkling. "Rub the magic crystal ball and get your peppermints." Linnie giggled and stretched out one finger, barely touching the shiny skin. Then she jerked the hand back and buried it in the skirt of her pinafore.

Mr. Darcy pretended to frown. "Felt like a fly up there," he said. "Can't make much magic with a touch like that."

Foolishness, thought Garrett, as he watched the postmaster hand out two flat, round candies, striped pink and white. One went directly into Linnie's mouth and the other into Stuffed Mabel's bloomers for safekeeping. Two pieces: everyone spoiled Linnie. For an awful moment Garrett thought that Mr. Darcy might give him a peppermint, too; the big man was studying his face in a peculiar way. But then Mr. Darcy laughed and clapped Garrett on the shoulder.

"Seems like just the other day you were her size and I pulled that stunt on you," he said. "Sometimes I forget about you bein' the man and all, now."

Garrett stood straighter. "Say thanks for the candy," he said to Linnie's ear, and then, to Mr. Darcy, "Did we get a letter?"

The postmaster scratched his broad nose and shook his head. "Not from your dad, if that's what you mean. You have to remember what shape the mail's in over there. And then you're one of the lucky ones, anyway. Some folks haven't heard from their boys at all since we went into France." Garrett smiled inside himself, where Mr. Darcy couldn't see. A lot of people talked about the war as if they were fighting it themselves; he had noticed that. "Fiddlers haven't heard one scrap from Roger," Mr. Darcy went on. "They sure would like to know if he's dead or alive, and I keep tellin' them no news is good news."

Garrett nodded. He knew better than to complain. One scary, terrible week in June the Allies had landed in Normandy to try to save Europe from that crazy Hitler; and for a while it seemed as if all the people he knew had been holding their breath to see who was going to live through it and who wasn't. There had been two letters from his father since then, from somewhere in France, Garrett supposed, although his father wasn't allowed to say where.

"Okay, Mr. Darcy, thanks."

"Well, don't rush off, Garrett. I didn't mean your box was empty. Look here." Beaming, Mr. Darcy filled Garrett's hands. "There's a pension check for Leo—make sure you hang on tight to that—and a bill for your poor mother to pay. And there's a few things for Em, too." All of a sudden the skin on his forehead wrinkled like an accordion. "Say, while you're deliverin' messages, I think you better give one to the Allen boy and those other fellas."

Garrett shifted his weight uneasily. "Okay, sure. What?"

"Whatever the bunch of you is up to I don't know, and don't care to," Mr. Darcy said slowly. "But whatever— you better take it easy on old Jack. He come in here this morning fit to be tied. Looked wild out of his eyes. Carried on so I like to never got the mail sorted. Boys been messin' in his garden, he said, and all around his garage and everything." The postmaster shook his head, and his eyes were troubled. "Wouldn't do for one of you kids to get hurt, you know it?"

"Jack Tramp wouldn't hurt anybody," Garrett protested. "He's harmless. Granpop said so." But there was a new feeling down the back of his neck, part excitement, part something else.

"Well, whatever. Just you remember." Mr. Darcy sighed and then returned to beaming, an expression suitable to his sun-round face.

"Good-by," said Garrett. "And thanks. Come on, Linnie." He reached for her hand, but no hand was there. "Linnie!"

She was already gone. Hiding in a bush, Garrett guessed, talking to herself and not caring about anything but Stuffed Mabel and her peppermints. At least once a week she disappeared that way, was searched out, scolded, and occasionally spanked. But nothing kept her from vanishing the next time she had the notion. At home, at least, Garrett knew where to find her, but here the looking would be harder. Brat! he thought. Little pest!

"Linnie! Linnie!" He walked back and forth and up and down at the crossroads, calling till his mouth was puckered dry in the heat. What if she wandered out in the road and got herself run over? "Linnie! Linnie!"

And as always, in her own sweet time, she answered him and came out of hiding and let him lead her home.

CHAPTER 3

On the far side of Jack Tramp's garden was Mr. Murdock's back lot, grown full of nettles and thistles and Queen Anne's lace. It was perfect natural cover, Stanley Middleton said, and the perfect place to hide his army.

"Keep your head down, McKay, and don't louse things up." Stanley crouched beside Garrett's place, going over the plan in detail. As if I couldn't remember anything, Garrett thought resentfully. As if I wasn't the Intelligence Officer, for pete's sake.

For two or three days after he had told them about Jack Tramp really having Hitler's first name, he had felt like a hero. "How do you like that?" they had said to one another. "He's a Nazi, for real!" Beanie Grant had peeled a gummed-paper star off an old arithmetic test and fastened it to Garrett's shirt pocket, and David Ray had made up a chant: *Garrett found a kraut / Garrett found a kraut / Hey there, Adolf / The kraut's found out!*

Jack Tramp's place had been the battleground all along, and the object of the game was to see him come out of his house in a rage, cursing and shaking his fists. They agreed it was the most entertaining thing in Merrittsburg, watching Jack carry on. Sometimes they even had made believe he was Hitler himself, just for the sake of the game. If anyone happened to hit old Jack directly with any of the things they used for ammunition, that would automatically kill the Führer and win the whole war. So far no one had ever dared throw right at him. Today, Garrett thought, someone probably would. Now that they were all thinking about how Jack's name connected him with the Germans, the game seemed more than fun—almost a patriotic duty.

"Wait for the signal," Stanley reminded Garrett, curling back his upper lip like a comic-book gangster. The difference was, when Stanley did it, you could see his chipped front tooth. "Remember to aim for the water barrel, that's the target. Anything that gets under the cover makes a win for the Allies, just like that." He snapped his fingers softly. "You *can* throw that far, can't you?"

Garrett hid his reddening face in the weeds. It made him disgusted, the way Stanley never would let him forget who was the youngest and the weakest. Stanley and Clarence were so proud of their broadening shoulders that most days they went without their shirts and bragged about how many times they could chin themselves without stopping.

"Sure I can throw that far," Garrett said scornfully. He wished that his father would come home and teach him about short-wave radio, the way he had promised in one of his letters. That would show Stanley a thing or two.

When Stanley crawled off, Garrett peered out of the weeds to see if the others were in position. Clarence and Beanie were at opposite ends of the weed lot, as far apart as brothers could get, which was the way they wanted it. Stanley was to be at the corner of Jack's garden with his cousin Duane, who was visiting for the week and had to be in on everything. David Ray, the scout, was across the lane at the edge of the McKays' garden, between the sweet corn and the pole beans. If the artillery didn't bring Jack Tramp out of his house, and if the rotten tomato bomb failed too, then it was David Ray's job to dart into his yard, pound on the door, and disappear. If anyone could get away with that, David Ray could.

Garrett sat back on his heels, half dreaming in spite of the prickling of thistles. The air around him was hot and still, almost heavy enough to touch; a bug droned uncomfortably close to his ear. He wished that he could trade skins with David Ray for a while. That would make him nearly a year older all at once—not much taller but a whole lot quicker on his feet. And daring. David Ray could climb to the top of the Stones at the creek without looking at his feet. Garrett couldn't even climb the trees in the apple orchard without getting sweaty all over. Aunt Em said that proved he was cautious and deliberate and intelligent. Stanley said it proved he was a coward.

"Fire one!" Clarence's voice rose out of the weeds. "Everybody throw!" Garrett lobbed his first shell. The green apple supply had run out; today's ammunition was mud balls, carefully rolled and dried ahead of time. Garrett hoped Aunt Em wouldn't pay much attention to the insides of his pockets when she washed his pants.

"Fire two!" On the signal he threw again, harder. The corner of Jack's garage was in his way, so that he had to throw over the end of the roof. And then he couldn't see if he'd hit anything.

Garrett fired again and again, blindly. There were soft thudding sounds; somebody was hitting something. He was tensed for a sign that Jack had been roused from his afternoon's nap, but he heard only the muffled thumping and

the boys rustling in the weeds. And Jefferson barking.
Jefferson belonged to Clarence and Beanie, more or less.
In truth, he was a wanderer who snuffled from back door
to back door with his ribs sticking out, hoping for some-
thing. Shut up, Jefferson, Garrett thought. Go chase Mrs.
Tanner's cat.

"Keep firing, you guys! Don't let up!" Clarence's head
showed for a moment above the weeds.

Just as Garrett threw with both hands at once, using the
last of his ammunition, there came the sound of shattering
glass. He caught his breath and held it. Jefferson quit his
barking. For a moment the afternoon was still. After lightning, everything waits for thunder.

Beanie yelled first. "He's comin' out! I see him!"

"Let's move!" Stanley cried. He ran for the edge of the
lane where the bicycles lay. "Retreat! Double time! Move
out!"

Garrett heard David Ray's back fender rattling against
the brace and felt a jealousy born of desperation. He had
no bicycle for making a getaway by the lane, and if he
tried to get directly home, he'd have to go through Jack's
yard, or his garden, or in plain sight of both. Wings would
serve better than wheels, he thought, and scrunched up
small among the weedstalks while he decided what to do.

At that moment Jack Tramp came hurrying around his
garage and past the corner of Mr. Murdock's lot, so close
that Garrett could see the garden mud caked on the old
man's clodhopper shoes. Two steps beyond Garrett's hiding place he halted.

"Damn kids!" he shouted harshly, and then his voice
sank to muttering. Garrett tried to hold his breath against
the powerful odor of the man's presence—a sour cabbage

smell of cigar smoke, unwashed clothing, and liniment. All he could see of Jack was his trouser cuffs, frayed and shiny with dirt, but he knew well enough what the rest looked like: tattered undershirt, gray suspenders, square jaw with stubble beard, fierce light blue eyes blinking out of deeply wrinkled sockets, straw hat pulled down on white hair.

Suddenly the old man shouted, "Hey! Get back here, you Grant boy! I see you sneakin'! You get back here!" The big shoes clumped off, following the bicycle tracks in the lane.

Garrett risked putting his head above the weeds, took one quick look and sank down flat because his knees wouldn't hold him. Jack Tramp had a shotgun. With a lump in his throat that felt bigger than Stanley's rotten tomato, Garrett listened to the old man's footsteps. When it seemed sure that he would not turn back, Garrett hauled himself out of Murdock's weeds and ran for his life, straight home across the road without looking right or left for traffic. Better to be run over by George Fisher's pickup than cut down by a blast from harmless old Jack Tramp's gun.

At supper that evening, Garrett studied his mother's face, and Granpop's and Aunt Em's, willing them not to ask him what he'd done with his afternoon. He wouldn't lie if asked. David Ray said that not only was Garrett the worst liar ever, he even sounded guilty when he was telling the truth. But he didn't intend to speak up about it, either. The only comfort he could find in the whole situation was knowing that his mud balls surely hadn't been the ones to break Jack's window. In spite of what he'd told Stanley, he couldn't throw that far.

For a while the conversation turned safely on other things. Linnie wailed about having to eat green beans because the juice would make her bread and jam all soggy. Mom straightened that out by giving Linnie her beans in a sauce dish, meanwhile entertaining them all with a story about two of the women at work who had got into an argument over who made the best movies, Clark Gable or Humphrey Bogart. Aunt Em complained about her bunions. Finally Garrett began to relax enough to enjoy his supper.

"Storm in the air," said Granpop, slowly buttering his bread. Everything that Granpop ever did or said was calm and deliberate. Once Garrett had heard Aunt Em say that Granpop wouldn't move any faster than a walk "even if his pants were afire." Slowly Granpop shook his head, barely disturbing his short, wavy gray hair. "Dog days," he said. "The devil gets into all sorts of folks. Must be what got into old Jack this afternoon, anyway."

"What's the matter with Jack?" asked Garrett's mother.

Garrett tried to eat without making the slightest click or clatter; he was careful not to look up, not to attract the slightest bit of attention to himself.

Granpop smiled faintly and shook his head again. "He outdid himself today."

"Well, what did he do?" Mom demanded. "The poor old thing." Garrett wished she wouldn't sound so sympathetic, though it was like her. Aunt Em was always scolding his mother for having such a soft heart.

Granpop laid down his fork. "I'll tell you what he did—he carried his shotgun all over town looking for Harry Grant's oldest boy. Claims some kids broke his window and threw dirt all over his house—I don't know what all. But the only one he got sight of was the Grant boy, hightailing it on his bicycle. So he went after him."

Garrett quit chewing.

Aunt Em sniffed. "Whatever was he carrying that beat-up old gun for? Thought he'd scare someone to death, I suppose."

"Worse, maybe," Granpop said. "He went in the Post Office, finally, just carryin' on terrible. So Paul talked and talked, till I guess he was red in the face, to get Jack to lay down the gun, and then Paul looked it over."

Garrett's eyes grew round as the top of the jam jar.

"It was loaded all right," said Granpop. "All ready to shoot."

Garrett couldn't help the noise he made, like a drowning man fighting for one final gasp of air. But the sound went unremarked in the general surprise.

"Loaded!" Aunt Em stared at Granpop. "Why, the old fool! Just imagine! He'll end up put away at the County Farm if he's not careful—if I've said that once, I've said it a hundred times."

Garrett's mother's face had gone white as milk. "Wouldn't you think there were enough loaded guns in the world?" she said to no one in particular. Then she looked at Garrett. "Thank goodness you've got sense enough to stay out of things like that," she said, and her eyes jumped to Linnie's face. "The both of you stay close to home, you hear?"

Garrett nodded miserably. He knew he ought to tell them all about it, and he knew he wasn't going to do it. He felt very guilty and a little afraid and not at all sure what he meant to do. If the Chiefs of Staff came up with a new plan, the Intelligence Officer couldn't just desert, could he? After all, his father was fighting the Germans, too.

CHAPTER 4

The storm Granpop had predicted broke in the night. Lightning cracked the dark bowl of the sky, rain slammed against the bedroom window. Linnie crawled onto the foot of her brother's bed and slept there, with Stuffed Mabel for a pillow. By morning, all Garrett could remember of it was tucking up his knees to make room and stopping his ears against the whimpering and the thunder.

Early chores had to be done in a wet new world. Where the chicken yard had been, a great puddle lay and the coop stood rimmed with mud, marooned. Another pool had formed at the low end of the pasture, and Elm Creek came out of its banks and across the corn rows to meet it.

Garrett was eager to get a closer look at the water in the field, to see how deep it was. He did his work in record time, in bare feet with his pants rolled up: corn for the chickens, water for the cow, a trip to the house with Granpop's pail of warm milk to be poured into the fat round crock in the pantry. When the cream rose, Aunt Em would skim it off and put it by, rattling things in the refrigerator as she tried to make room.

"I'll be down over the pasture hill, Aunt Em!" he called.

Aunt Em had Linnie on her lap in the kitchen rocker.

When Linnie saw Garrett she tried to pull away from the brush that her aunt was using on her tangled curls. "Me too!" she crowed. "Me too, over the pasture hill!"

Aunt Em snorted. "Indeed not. You screech when there's three inches of water in the washtub. What if you fell in the deep? And you be careful, too, Garrett. High water's full of surprises."

He nodded and let the screen door slam, with Aunt Em calling her cautions after him. "And you mind what your mother said, Garrett! Don't you wander over there by Jack's place!"

If she said more, he didn't hear it. David Ray Allen was waiting for him on the well curb, grinning over a hulk of rusty metal.

"What's *that?*" asked Garrett for greeting—though, plainly enough, *that* was a gasoline tank. "You been sneaking things off Fiddler's scrap pile again?"

David Ray grinned his famous grin, the one that squeezed his freckles into a solid patch of orange. "Can't you tell a U.S. submarine when you see one? There's an ocean waiting, McKay! We can help General MacArthur go after Manila or something."

"O-*kay!*" Garrett bounced a little, from wet feet and excitement. It was good to have something new to do, a relief. The war game at Jack's could never be quite the same after yesterday, and he was glad that David Ray seemed to realize it. Garrett whistled his way through the sodden pasture, remembering other times when the water had risen above the cornfield. Once, when his father had not been in the Army, they had built a toy raft and sailed it. As he remembered it, they had played with the raft for days and days, but there might have been just one afternoon, or even one hour. It was funny about good times, how they seemed like forever when you thought back about them. In truth, he knew, the waters of Elm Creek could rise with surprising speed and drain away just as fast.

David Ray launched the old tank and Garrett quit trying to figure out whether his memory tricked him. "She floats!" cried David Ray. "I'm an admiral!"

When they balanced it carefully, the shaky craft would support both boys at once. The tank was big, and patched in several places—Garrett wondered whose truck it had come from. It was flat enough to sit on, though not very comfortably, and it kept getting stuck in the wire fence along the cornfield. They might have made a real game of naval operations if all their attention had not been claimed by the effort to stay upright.

"This can be a carrier—" David Ray began, and just then fell into the water. He came up spluttering and covered with mud, clowning. That was David Ray for you, thought Garrett, laughing. David Ray was always making people laugh. It was one of the things Garrett missed about his father—the wild and funny antics, everyone laughing. Aunt Em would try to act proper and scandalized, but in the end she'd laugh the loudest. Mom would say, "You clown," and smile in a special slow way she had, and often as not his father would quit whatever he was doing and hug her. Once he had hugged her so hard that he lifted her right off the floor; afterward, she had worn tape around her middle till the doctor from Springtown said her broken rib was healed.

Now David Ray was making faces and calling, "Step right up, folks! See the one and only swamp monster of Elm Creek. He who slept peacefully for generations in the muddy bottoms rises to strike terror in your hearts! Donations accepted! Right this way, folks!" He was trailing drowned weeds and storm-blown leaves; his cheerful red hair was saddened with mud. Garrett held the tank firmly to escape the same fate, but he couldn't stop laughing. He didn't want to. It was wonderful to laugh, even when you were all doubled over with an aching side.

While they laughed, there were shouts upstream and Stanley Middleton came into view, leading the Grant brothers through water that swirled about their thighs. As if someone had pressed an invisible switch, David Ray ceased to be Garrett's special companion and became one of the others. The swamp monster of Elm Creek disappeared in a shake and a swipe, leaving behind an ordinary, mud-streaked boy.

"Don't hog the boat, McKay," said David. "Get off and give the other guys a chance."

Garrett scowled and landed himself on a huge round stone at the corner of the fence row. "It'll never hold Clarence," he said.

Clarence had the longest legs of any boy that Garrett knew. Mr. Medary at the high school could hardly wait for him to get another year older so that he could be made into a basketball player. From the back, Clarence looked like a grown man, though his face was a boy's face. He had grown up breathing through his mouth so that now his lips habitually hung slack, and some people thought he wouldn't have brains enough to be on the basketball team. But Garrett knew that was unfair; Clarence's mind was quick enough. He even hoped, himself, to grow to be something like Clarence. Sometimes he hung by his arms from the lowest limb of the maple tree by the road, trying to get stretched. But Garrett covered his admiration with scorn, the same as the other boys.

"When you get on that boat, Clarence," he said, "it's going straight to the bottom."

Clarence's brother giggled.

Clarence looked at Garrett with the passing interest due a fly about to be swatted. "Go hang," he said in a pleasant voice. But when Clarence got on top of the tank, it rode just below the water, slowly filled itself, and sank. The big boy swore. They all laughed and Garrett, as one of them, felt uncommonly bold.

"This is more fun than going after old Jack Tramp," he said suddenly. "We won't have to do that any more." He looked from one face to another, testing.

Beanie quit giggling and ducked his head; Stanley and David Ray began to fuss with the tank, draining it; Clarence twisted up his face and stared at nothing. Immediately Garrett felt himself apart again—alone, confused.

"What's the matter with all you guys?" he demanded.

"Just shut up about the old Nazi, huh?" Clarence said.

Beanie looked up with a wise smile. "Some things Clarence don't even want *mentioned*."

"Shut up, you dummy."

Beanie giggled. "You didn't hear about it, did you, Garrett? Old Jack the Kraut came and told Dad that Clarence broke his window, so Dad gave him money to get some new glass, but he said he was going to take it out of Clarence's hide. And did he ever!"

"It's time you paid your own share, you big mouth." Beanie's brother leaned toward him, grabbing for his hair. As he bent, Clarence's pants and wet shirt slid apart. Garrett saw the strap marks then, red and blue as a flag. He had to look away. The injustice of it was enormous, and he struggled for something to say—something comforting, but with dignity. Yet if such words existed they kept escaping him, the way Beanie again and again slithered out of his brother's grasp.

"That dirty old Nazi," was all that Garrett could find to say. Jack Tramp hadn't laid the strap on Clarence's back, but in a roundabout way everything seemed to come back to him, back to the hatefulness he stood for. Back to Adolf Hitler himself, making a war and turning everyone's life all upside down.

"Garr-ett!" Aunt Em's voice suddenly broke through the sound of the boys' splashing. "Come on up to the house and eat! I like to hollered my lungs out." She appeared at the top of the slope, puffing and cross, her apron hem spattered. "The rest of you boys quit that fighting and carrying on and get home and make yourselves useful. Thank fortune there'll soon be school to keep you out of trouble."

The four boys left him all at once; united by Aunt Em's attack, they moved off in closed ranks. Only David Ray broke formation, to push their rusty boat into a clump of weeds beyond the fence row. It didn't matter, Garrett supposed. Already the water was lower, and no one could float on mud. He stared after them, and then up the slope toward Aunt Em. Oh, how he wished—but he didn't quite know for what. If only his father could come home.

CHAPTER 5

Summer was slippery as a catfish, Granpop said. You thought you had it, and then it was gone. That was true enough when you were thinking about how many days of vacation were left, Garrett could see that. But if you measured time by the Post Office, summer crawled along like cold molasses. Not once during August was there a letter from his father, and the waiting from one day to the next seemed to grow longer and longer.

Sometimes Garrett wondered if anyone cared as much as he did. Granpop never complained about anything, and Aunt Em's usual reply to a question about his father was a glare. "Don't ask *me* about him, child," she would say. "Only the Lord knows what he's doing by now." As for Linnie, she didn't think about Dad at all. When Garrett tried to talk to her about him, her eyes would frost over like a pitcher of cold lemonade on a hot day and she would go off in a corner with Stuffed Mabel to look at the Sears and Roebuck catalog.

Even Mom didn't say much about the waiting and the wondering; Garrett supposed maybe she was too busy and too tired all the time to be as lonesome for Dad as he was. But then one day when he needed shoelaces, she sent him to the top drawer of the chest in her room to look for a new pair, and what he found was a little calendar with a leather cover like a book. All the empty boxes that stood for the days of August had zeroes in them. Zero, no letter. Zero, no Dad. It made Garrett cold and warm at the same time, just looking at it.

Labor Day came and Garrett's mother didn't have to work. It was the last day before school, and the sun nearly burst itself shining.

"We ought to have a picnic," Mom said. "There's cold meat in the fridge for sandwiches—I could do a chicken but that would take too long. And there's half the sour cream cake from yesterday—" She ticked off the menu on her fingers. "I could make some lemonade—it's too much sugar, I know, but it's a holiday, after all. And I'll make a few deviled eggs."

Granpop laid aside his magazine and beamed, his eyes disappearing at the corners in a web of wrinkles. "At the Stones, Jane?" he asked. "The way we used to do?"

Garrett looked from one to the other, holding his breath, remembering. Summer picnics, his father whistling, Aunt Em giggling like a girl. Once Garrett had ridden all the way to the Stones on his father's shoulders, and Granpop had carried their lunch in a grocery sack. That was because Mom had put Linnie in the picnic basket, tiny Linnie, mewing like a new kitten.

Granpop rubbed his chin. "You sure now, Jane? I thought you might want to ease up on things today, rest a little, have some time to yourself."

She shook her head. "We have to have a little fun, all of us."

Linnie bounced around the kitchen, excited. "I'm going,

too?" she begged. "Me too? And Stuffed Mabel? How about Stuffed Mabel, Mom?"

"Of course, you too," Mom laughed. "And even Stuffed Mabel. You can pack her a lunch if you want—pebble soup or mud pie or something special like that." Linnie squealed so that Mom held her ears. "Listen, Garrett," she said above the noise, "you run over to Em's and see if she feels like going with us."

Garrett ran, and Aunt Em wanted to go. She didn't say it in so many words, but Garrett could tell.

"What a fool idea," was what she said. "Down there with all those bugs and prickle-burrs and poison ivy and slippery rocks and God-knows-what-all. Too hot in the sun, too cool in the shade, too damp to sit." She frowned at Garrett, who was grinning at her. "Well—tell your mother I'll bring some of the green tomato pickle."

Garrett was first in line along the creek toward the Stones, making a path for his mother and Em and Granpop and for Linnie, who had to come last because she stopped so often to look at things on the ground. Stuffed Mabel had been put in with the sandwiches to leave Linnie's hands free for poking. "See it!" she would cry. "See this!" And anyone walking behind would have fallen right over her. Far in the rear came the Grants' dog, Jefferson, with his nose to the picnic scent.

"We've got us a regular parade," Granpop said and began to whistle "The Stars and Stripes Forever." They joined in one by one until Linnie's attempt came out more of a moan than a whistle and set the dog to howling in sympathy. After that they were all laughing too hard to pucker, which put an end to the whistling.

Garrett led on, fighting through the nettles on an over-grown path along the creek bank. Above them towered the Stones themselves, great blocks in a solid stack as long as Granpop's barn and higher, though not half as wide. At one end, footed deep in a great mound of earth, the un-finished abutment rose unevenly to its flat top, like the staircase of a wild sky-giant. The other end reached just beyond the edge of the lower bank, with an outcropping of smaller, square-cut rocks built up to a rough ledge sev-eral feet above the line of the water. All around the base were huge blocks that once had been part of the Stones but had fallen long ago and now were sunk at odd angles into the yielding earth.

When they had made their way around the high ground at the upland end of the Stones and could see the other side, Linnie shrieked with delight. They were close enough to see the picnic stone, which lay quite flat between two fallen tree trunks, like a table with benches. She skipped through the tangled growth at her feet, back and forth along the side of the Stones, patting them, chittering to herself, testing the surfaces, sniffing things. Just like Jeffer-son, Garrett thought. Little kids were just like dogs, grub-bing along with their noses close to the ground. But his nose, too, was filled up with the smell of the place: damp stone and green moss, dead wood and growing weeds, creek water.

"I'm starved," he said.

"Me and Stuffed Mabel are thirsty," called Linnie.

"In a minute, okay?" Mom rummaged through the basket. "Just hold your horses."

Aunt Em was spreading the checkered picnic cloth and covering the cool moss of the near log with several thicknesses of newspaper. She was bound to sit in a dry spot. "Linnie, don't you go near the edge—you hear?"

"Such a fuss," Granpop said gently, easing his body down to sit on the roots of an elm. "Was peaceful here till we came." He looked over the fallen stones and the slow, sun-marked water. "I ought to have brought my pole," he said. "There's catfish on yon side of the riffles."

Garrett helped himself to an egg. "Want me to go get your pole, Granpop?" He hoped that Granpop would tell him to go get two poles, and then they would both sit with their feet dangling over the bank and their thoughts drifting like twigs in the current. But Granpop said no, it was too much bother.

"You might as well go, Garrett," Mom said. "I forgot cups for the lemonade."

He took another egg and started running, crashing back the way they had come. "Be right back!" he called with his mouth full.

"Mind you don't bring the good cups," Aunt Em called after him, and her voice was softened and muffled, almost lost between the trees and the Stones.

When Garrett got to the barn he was panting, and he was glad that Stanley wasn't around to laugh. "You're soft, McKay," Stanley would say. "You're a marshmallow." But he didn't let himself think about it.

Garrett took two fishing poles from their place on the wall inside the barn, sneezing once in the hay-dusty air. Then he hurried toward the house to get cups for the picnic lemonade. His tongue and his throat were aching for a cool taste of it, and he couldn't see why the hens had to slow him down so in the chicken yard, squawking and flapping around his feet. "Dumb clucks," he muttered at them.

"Shut up, you dumb clucks. Did old Jefferson come up here and get you all riled up?"

Garrett turned to look for the dog; he was sure that Jefferson was responsible for the hens' disorder. But what he saw was a stranger, a plain-looking man in a cap with a black visor, peering into the house through one of the kitchen windows. Garrett felt as if someone had slipped a caterpillar down his shirt collar.

"Hey!" he said, and his voice quivered more than he wanted.

"Hi, there!" The stranger seemed relieved to have been discovered. "This is the McKay place, isn't it?" He had a pale yellow envelope in one hand. "I began to think no one was home, with this a holiday and all."

For the first time Garrett saw a shiny black fender and a glare of chrome from the unfamiliar car in the driveway.

"Well, son?" The man frowned at Garrett. "Tell me if this is the McKays'." He glanced at the envelope. "Is Mrs. Jane McKay here? I've got this to deliver to her."

A telegram. Only bad news came by telegram. There was a buzzing in Garrett's head that stopped up his ears.

"She's down there by the creek," he said. "We're having a picnic."

The delivery man looked at his feet. "Well," he said, "I'm supposed to personally see that she gets this."

Garrett had a quick picture of how it would be—his mother fixing Linnie's plate and Granpop dreaming over the fishing spot and the stranger coming into their midst. Aunt Em would be talking, and she would stop.

"I'll take it down for you," Garrett said. "She's my mother."

The man rubbed his chin. "I shouldn't," he said. He

looked at his pocket watch. "But then again, that looks like a long walk, and I've got to get back to town. Make sure she gets it right away, all right?" He turned and went toward his car. When he walked, one leg was stiff. "Thanks, boy," he said over his shoulder. "Appreciate it."

Garrett nodded and laid the two fishing poles in the grass. He walked right through the complaining chickens without hearing them. He felt numb all over, every inch of him as dead as his jaw had been when the dentist in Springtown pulled his bad tooth. He walked across the barn lot and over the pasture hill, through the trees along Elm Creek to the Stones.

Linnie wailed when she saw him. "Where's my cup?" she demanded. "I'm thirsty and so's Mabel. Mabel needs a drink really *bad*."

Granpop's forehead showed an extra crease. "Couldn't find the poles either, huh?"

Garrett shook his head and gave the envelope to his mother. He didn't really look at her. "There was a Western Union man up at the house," he said.

Then he moved off to be by himself. He stood near the corner of the Stones and stared at the water. Sunshine was yellow, according to one of the poems in the fifth-grade reader, but he could see that it wasn't true. Sunshine came in lots of colors—deep green among the trees, golden brown on the water, a terrible glaring blue in the sky. He concentrated on the sunshine as if his life depended on it.

Garrett's mother cleared her throat. "Andy's missing in action," she said in a tight, terrible voice.

Linnie began to cry. "I'm thirsty," she whined. "I want my lemonade."

But none of them paid her the least bit of attention.

CHAPTER 6

That fall the maple tops glowed like firelight on a stick; their bright leaves were sparks in the wind. Birds arranged themselves on the telephone wires to play follow-the-leader going south. At nine each weekday morning school began, and every Friday without fail there was a spelling test. September turned into October, the same as always. How could it be, thought Garrett, that the season went on as if nothing had happened?

Preacher Martin came to offer them comfort while Mom was at work and Aunt Em was busy scrubbing the kitchen. It was Granpop he talked to, and they talked for a long time. When he left, Granpop shook his hand and said, "You're always welcome here, Reverend, you know that," and Preacher Martin said, "You're always welcome in church, too." Granpop nodded and smiled, but he never went.

Mom said that there was no need to believe the worst, not yet, not even when the day of the telegram was long past and no word had come to contradict it. "We'll just keep believing he's all right," she said. But her voice reminded Garrett of Gracie Dean reciting "October's Bright Blue Weather" at assembly.

Sometimes at night, after Garrett was sure that Linnie was asleep, he would reach over to the nightstand for his father's photograph and tuck it under his blanket. With the frame poking him in the ribs and his eyes tight shut, he could remember special things. There was one Christmas, for instance, when he was sick with the chicken pox and not allowed outside, so his father had built him a snowman just beneath the window where he could reach out and touch it.

Another winter, he remembered, there wasn't any snow at all, but he had his heart set on snowballs. His father said they'd have to make do, and so they had a mud-ball fight instead. Afterward Aunt Em had chased them out of the kitchen, yapping and scolding, and then Garrett's father had hit her with a mud ball—*squash!*—on the front of her clean apron. "You may be big as a horse, Andy McKay," Aunt Em had spluttered, "but you're still a pup—and you'd better learn not to fool with an old dog!" And then Garrett had watched, unbelieving, while Aunt Em stuck out one leg so far that it showed the rolled-down top on her stocking, pushed his father off balance, and rubbed his nose in the mud. Dad had picked himself up, laughing, and pinched Em's cheek with his gooey fingers. "You win, old girl," was what he had said. Garrett still marveled at it: even Granpop dared not call Aunt Em "old girl."

Would there ever be good times like that again? Sometimes, with one finger, Garrett would trace the frame of the photograph, imagining that he could see the outline of the face. If only he could believe that his father would come home, ever. People around town talked as if he was dead already. It made Garrett feel sick, just thinking about it, but it was hard to put out of one's mind—the idea of his father lying all twisted up and still as a stone in a ditch somewhere, like a picture he had seen in *Life* magazine.

There was only one small compensation for the fact that his father was missing: it gave him new stature among the boys. There was a certain look of respect now in Stanley Middleton's eyes, and Beanie sometimes asked him to play catch or monkey-move-up without insisting on a bribe from Garrett's lunch box. David Ray waited by the Post Office every morning so they could walk together to school. The war game at Jack Tramp's place had been ended by unspoken agreement, but they still talked about the old man.

"I don't see how you stand it," David Ray confided, "living with that old Nazi right in sight." Beanie suggested that he was probably a spy, planning to blow up something vital, like the aircraft plant on the other side of Springtown. Beanie had a lot of ideas like that, and David Ray told them around the playground as if they were true stories. David Ray was such a good storyteller that Garrett, who didn't believe one word he was saying, still began to feel that it would be a good thing if Jack Tramp would just disappear off the face of the earth.

Then one Sunday morning when the leaves were almost gone and the stragglers among the birds were calling goodby, Jack Tramp presented himself at the McKays' back door. "You hear anything yet?" he asked abruptly when Granpop answered his knock.

For a moment Granpop looked puzzled, and then he shook his head. "From Andy, you mean. Not a word, no. It's still up in the air. He's still missing, as far as we know."

Jack Tramp grunted. "Too bad," he said, and turned around and walked away.

"How do you like that?" Mom said, moving toward the door and looking after him. "That was a nice thing for him to do, taking the trouble to ask. He does scare me with that gun of his, but I feel sorry for him—poor old man stuck over there in that lonesome old shack. We ought to ask him to eat with us."

Garrett put down the flashlight he was trying to fix. She wouldn't, he thought. But Granpop had killed a hen and Aunt Em had made an extra big batch of noodles, and Mom's face was set.

"And you children could be nice to him," she went on. "He wouldn't act so much like a wild thing if he was treated with respect."

Aunt Em muttered over the soup pot like a witch brewing charms. "You know how he is, Jane," she said. "Not sociable one bit. Never was. We could send him his dinner on a tray and let him eat whenever he had the notion. I could smell his cigar clear in here, and he wasn't even inside the door."

Mom sighed and pushed a strand of hair—fine and brown and straight like Garrett's—away from her face. She went back to her pan of potatoes, hacking away at each one as if it had to be killed before the skin would come off. "I guess I thought he'd just fill up the empty space for once," she said.

Granpop didn't say a word, but he put on his jacket and walked over to Jack Tramp's house.

And so Jack Tramp came to Sunday dinner. Linnie hid in one corner of the kitchen, behind the opened dining room door. No amount of coaxing would bring her out. Finally Mom told Garrett to leave her alone. "No tapioca pudding for people who won't sit at the table," she said loudly. But Linnie stayed in the corner, quiet as a puff of dust, and dinner started without her.

The old man sat stiffly at the dining room table, avoiding contact with the Sunday cloth and, as much as possible, with Great-grandma Franklin's silver. Garrett sat across from him and tried not to stare, the way he would at a woolly worm or a hairy spider. Jack was cleaner than usual, Garrett noted, with a dark sweater buttoned over his undershirt, and his hair stuck so tight to his head that it might have been varnished. Could there truly be some connection between Jack Tramp and Hitler's army, Garrett wondered? Might he really be a spy, or a saboteur, waiting for the right moment to set dynamite to the B & O tracks? Ridiculous, insisted Garrett's head. Jack Tramp had lived in Merrittsburg for years and years. But his skin went right on prickling at the sight of a man named Adolf Schilling sitting in his father's place.

"You been feeling all right, Jack?" queried Aunt Em, who kept dabbing her nose with her napkin. In spite of the fact that there was no cigar in sight, Jack Tramp smelled the same as ever. "You look peaked—you know that?"

He shook his head and mumbled something between bites of mashed potato, which he ate with a great smacking sound.

"Seconds, Jack?" Mom offered him the platter of chicken, and Garrett was annoyed at the way he took the last drumstick and let it plop into the noodles on his plate. Splatters of broth fell onto the tablecloth. Aunt Em frowned, but his mother smiled—the way she sometimes smiled at Linnie, Garrett thought, as if there weren't any rules. "Eat all you want," Mom said. "There's plenty."

Granpop made small talk about the weather while Jack

went on chewing and smacking with an occasional nod of the head to show that he was listening. After a time, little spikes of hair came unstuck and bristled around his face so that he looked like the ugly troll in Linnie's picture book about the three billy goats. When he had cleaned his plate, wiping it dry with a bit of bread, he pushed back his chair and got up. No one else had finished.

"Surely you aren't going," Mom said. "There's pudding for dessert, and molasses cookies."

"Don't want any," said Jack Tramp gruffly. "Sweets make poison in your body. Rot your insides." He looked directly at Garrett, and waggled one finger. "You better not eat candy, boy. Won't grow right. Won't get tall like young Andy."

Garrett struggled with a mouthful of noodles and wished he could think of some brilliant reply. But he couldn't. The old man began shuffling away from the table.

"Stay and visit a spell," Granpop suggested.

"Can't. Got things to do." Jack Tramp's words popped out of his mouth like small explosions. Probably he was going home to make a few bombs, Garrett thought. Fix up a few grenades. Something. As Jack went past the dining room door there was a faint scraping sound. The door moved an inch, perhaps two.

"What's that? Huh? What we got here?" He swung the door wide and leaned around it, peering into the corner.

Linnie screamed and the old man jumped.

"What's wrong with her?" he demanded, backing off toward the kitchen door. Linnie caught her breath and wailed again.

"What's the matter?" Jack repeated. "She crazy or something?"

Aunt Em pushed past Mom. "Linnie, hush up!" she commanded, and she glared at Jack Tramp. "You frightened her half to death, that's all. She's shy."

Shy! Garrett began to laugh to himself; it took real control not to choke on the last of his dinner. Old Jack was hustling backward across the kitchen like someone in a Mickey Mouse cartoon, Linnie was screeching at full power, and Mom and Aunt Em were all tangled up trying to get to her.

Jack let himself out the back door. "Good eats!" he called from the back porch. "Much obliged!" The door slammed after him.

"Oh, Linnie," Mom kept saying. "Just look at you!"

Garrett got up quietly and peered at his sister through the crack between the hinges. Her socks were wet, her shoes were wet, the floor was wet.

"Imagine!" Aunt Em said, shocked. Her nose twitched. "Just imagine—at your age!"

Garrett went back to his chair and began slowly to finish his dinner. Once, just after he had started his first year of school, he had been standing in the hall waiting his turn for a drink when the bell for fire drill—he had never heard it before—started gonging right above his head. "Lookit!" someone had yelled. "Garrett jist peed himself." He remembered the wet, warm surprise of it, and the giggles that followed him out into the schoolyard. While his class waited for the all-clear bell, his legs had got frightfully cold.

Poor Linnie. After she changed her clothes he might read to her, or push her in the swing, or let her play Chinese checkers with his set. Or then again he might not. She didn't have to poke herself off behind that door in the first place, did she? She didn't have to be such a complete crybaby about everything. Garrett knew for sure how he felt about Jack Tramp, but about Linnie he was never quite able to make up his mind.

CHAPTER 7

On Monday morning Garrett was so slow getting to school that David Ray had gone on without him. But his class was dismissed for noon recess a few minutes early and he hurried to be first at the boys' meeting place. In the far corner of the schoolyard beyond the athletic field stood a weathered frame building used for storage, with a pile of scrap lumber behind it. This place the boys had claimed for their own. It was out of sight of the main playground and too far across the high grass for the teachers to come checking. Now and again girls came to spy around, but usually they got their arms twisted until they went shrieking back to the slide and the monkey-bars.

Once Beanie had found Annie Edwards behind the lumber pile all by herself. He said he had just tried to push her back where she belonged, but she told everyone that he had grabbed her skirt and pulled it up. Garrett didn't know which story to believe, but he knew for a fact that afterward Beanie had a double lump on his head like an oversized peanut to mark the place where Annie hit him with a chunk of two-by-four. Lately, however, no one had bothered them.

Garrett waved a greeting as the boys ambled in—David

Ray, Beanie and Georgie Lake, who rode the bus and never saw the others except at school. Clarence walked a good way behind, talking to Poke Adams. Neither one of them liked to be seen hanging around with younger boys all the time.

Stanley walked up to Garrett and made a face. He extended one hand as if it held a cup, with his little finger in an exaggerated curl. "Pass the sugar, please, Adolf," he said, in falsetto. "Pass the cream, please, Adolf—phaw!" He slapped his two hands together in disgust. "McKay," he said, "you stink. We heard about who you *entertained*, yesterday."

Garrett swallowed. "Yeah, well, it wasn't me that invited him."

"It doesn't figure," Beanie said. "You, of all people, having that old Nazi in for a meal."

"Of all people," echoed Georgie Lake, who hadn't any idea what they were talking about. He pursed his lips and pinched up his voice in a convincing imitation of Mrs. Thurman, the music teacher. "How could you do it, Garrett? How could you possibly?"

The others laughed and Garrett fought with his face, to keep it from showing his feelings.

"Cut it out, you guys," David Ray spoke up. He was walking back and forth, back and forth, balancing on a two-by-four that lay half hidden in the faded grass. "He's loyal," David said, executing a one-footed turn. "He's even going to prove it, right tonight."

"How's that?" asked Garrett, with a rush of grateful feeling. "What am I doing?" Whatever it was, it didn't matter. He couldn't let them think he was getting friendly with Jack Tramp.

"Meet me after school," David Ray said. "And the rest of you keep out of it," he warned. "It's private."

What Garrett was going to do, David Ray said as they hurried away from the schoolyard that afternoon, was help him win the monthly scrap-collecting contest. They were both shivering because the wind had turned chilly; Garrett's nose began to feel drippy.

"You have to be in seventh to be in the contest, right?" David Ray said reasonably. "So you aren't in for yourself, you might as well help me." He began to whistle between his teeth.

Garrett nodded, unimpressed. "Sure," he said. "I helped you last month anyway, don't you remember? Is that all I'm supposed to do?" He kicked at a stone and watched it bounce ahead. "I don't see what that's gonna prove. Just about everybody collects scrap stuff for the war."

David Ray whistled louder, the tune sounding a bit like "America" with a few bars of "The Star Spangled Banner" thrown in. "You'll see," he said to Garrett. "We can use your wagon, can't we?"

"No reason we can't," said Garrett with a shrug. Then he looked sharply at the other boy. "No fair going to Fiddler's," he said. "Mr. Boyd said it would be cheating—I heard him."

"I'm not going to Fiddler's," David Ray replied with exaggerated patience. "Don't you *trust* me?" His eyes were glinting like two twinkles on a Christmas tree, and Garrett tried without success to figure out what he was plotting. "I'll come by for you in half an hour."

At the Post Office the boys went their separate ways, and Garrett hurried home to change his clothes. He said hello to Aunt Em, ate two cookies that she gave him and two more when she wasn't looking, then got ready to go out.

"I'll be helping David Ray collect scrap," he said.

"You be back in time to help with the chores, you hear?" Aunt Em was bent over the ironing board, looking cross. The whole kitchen smelled of washday, soap and bleach and the steam of damp linen being flattened by Em's iron. Between two chairs was strung a thin rope decorated with damp socks, all at crazy angles. "Don't you run into Linnie's clothesline, either," she warned, resting the iron on its heel. "She fussed over it half the day, and the other half she just moped around."

Garrett had his coat on and his hand on the door.

"You might as well take her out, too," said Aunt Em. "She needs company."

"Aw—no!" Garrett was furious with himself. He ought to have been quicker. "She'll be in the way—she won't be able to keep up, probably." And he wasn't certain where they were going, but he didn't want to tell Aunt Em that. "She can't come," he said decisively.

"Can too! I can too!" Linnie herself tumbled out of one of her hiding places, a niche between the refrigerator and the end of the cupboards. She pulled her coat down from its low hook and put on her knitted hat backward. Its fuzzy red pompons rested on the nape of her neck, and the ties sprouted at the top of her head like little stringy horns.

"Do up her buttons," Aunt Em said. Aunt Em believed in economy with words as with everything; she would no sooner waste breath on an argument than throw away perfectly good, reusable items like waxed bread-wrappers or lengths of string or chipped jelly glasses. "I'm not of a mind to fuss with you, boy. Mrs. Tanner's been here half the afternoon—that woman does nothing but talk, talk, talk—so the work's not done, and supper's not started, and—" She glanced at the clock. "Go on now, and you keep a sharp eye on your sister."

David Ray, when he saw Linnie, was very much annoyed. He jammed his fists tight in his pockets and glared at Garrett, at the wagon he was pulling, and at Linnie, who was riding in it. Linnie was unaffected; she lay on her back with her knees pointing at the sky, talking to herself. Her eyes were squeezed shut; it was hard to tell who she was pretending to be, or where.

Garrett shrugged an apology. "Aunt Em said I had to."

"Well, for cripe's sake," David Ray said as he led off, "make sure she stays out of the way." When they turned into Jack Tramp's lane, Garrett thought that Linnie would jump out of the wagon and run home, but when she opened her eyes all she looked at was clouds.

"I see a fat sheep," she crooned to herself, "a fat sheep in the sky, sheep." She sang on and on without a tune.

David Ray stopped just past the edge of Mr. Murdock's back lot and directed Garrett to pull the wagon in among the tall, dry weedstalks.

"What for?" demanded Garrett. "If Mr. Murdock's got junk for you he'll have it in that shed up by his house."

There was a snuffling in the weeds that made David Ray jump, but he recovered himself at the sight of Jefferson's waving tail.

"Go home, you good-for-nothing dog," David said. "Go find Clarence." He slapped his leg. "Go home, boy. Attaway!" Jefferson wagged harder and approached the wagon.

"Cripes!" David Ray shook his head. "What a dumb dog."

The old hound dropped his snout over the side of the wagon and nosed Linnie's sleeve. She sat up, squealing a little. Now, Garrett felt sure, she was going to look around and start to cry. She didn't. Jefferson stared at her with his sad brown eyes and his mouth held slack as if he was grinning. The very tip of his tongue showed, and around his nose clung countless burrs and Spanish needles.

"Poor messy dog," said Linnie, and kissed him on one ear as she began to pick his coat clean. Aunt Em had better not ever find out about Linnie kissing a dog. Garrett didn't even want to think about what she would say.

David Ray turned his back on the wagon. "It's not Murdock's junk I'm after," he said. "I know where there's a stack of paper a mile high, plus two tons of old cans and stuff."

"Me too," Garrett said, sniffing with cold and disbelief. "Right up there in your imagination."

Suddenly the other boy broke into a grin so wide that his cheeks nearly covered up his eyes. "Have you ever looked through the window of Jack's garage?"

"David Ray Allen!" Garrett felt his heart thump. "He never said you could get anything out of his garage! I bet a million dollars."

"He didn't say I couldn't." David Ray stuck out his tongue and waggled it. "Now come on."

"You never even asked him," Garrett said flatly, knowing it was true.

David Ray looked at him with disgust. "Don't you see?" he said. "Don't you want to show the guys that you're not a friend of this old Nazi? It's gonna be funny, McKay. We take his scrap metal, see, and it gets made into shells and stuff to blast his ugly old German relations right off the face of the earth. Get it? Imagine this German soldier, see, all ready to throw a grenade right at—at your dad, Garrett, it *could* be, you know, it's still possible—and all of a sudden, BOOM! comes this direct hit and—*aaaaaagh!*" He staggered, clutching himself in pretended pain. "It's part of the war effort, you dummy."

Garrett shuddered, his imagination filling with the scene that his friend had created. His mouth felt dry and prickly, as if he had tried to chew on one of Mr. Murdock's brown thistle heads. "He keeps his garage locked," was what Garrett finally said. Jack Tramp had no car; for all Garrett knew he had never had one. The garage was a catchall. Once when the double doors had stood open Garrett had noticed several ladders, some buckets, and a rack of paintbrushes, plus a lot of junk.

David Ray straightened up and gave himself a shake. "No sir," he said. "He doesn't lock that little door in the back. It's just hooked with a wire. Come on."

Garrett followed, worrying. It must be wonderful, he thought, to be sure of everything the way David Ray was, to know what you were going to do and be daring enough to do it. The closer they came to the garage, the more uneasy Garrett felt and the damper his hands got. His mother would have a fit, and so would Granpop, probably. Not to mention Aunt Em.

"I'll wait here," he said, and stopped in the shelter of a lilac bush that had not lost its leaves. "I'll be lookout, and you bring the stuff this far and hand it to me and I'll take it back to the wagon." He was miserable as he said it,

thinking that going halfway was worse somehow than doing the wrong thing altogether. David Ray never did anything halfway.

"You baby," said David Ray. Garrett studied the buttons
on his coat front, avoiding the contempt in his friend's eyes.

David looked both ways, then crept across the narrow
open space to Jack Tramp's garage and let himself in the
door by drawing a stick upward through the crack. Garrett fidgeted, coughed, pulled his head down into his coat
like a turtle going into its shell. It was taking long enough,
he thought with a sour, hidden face. Probably David Ray
was really enjoying himself, poking through everything
before deciding what to carry out.

On the other side of the dusty window, David Ray's
bright hair bobbed and dipped, like a battle flag in enemy
territory. He was taking too long, Garrett thought, watching the corner of Jack's house anxiously. Too long, he
thought. Then he saw the old man.

Or he thought he saw him. There was a blur of dark
coat and white hair moving near the corner of the garage,
on the side where the double doors were.

"David Ray!" croaked Garrett. "David Ray, you better
come out of there!" After a moment David Ray disappeared from behind the window and came scuttling out the
little back door, his arms loaded with squashed tin cans.

"Hurry up!" urged Garrett, inching backward into the
weeds. "Hurry!"

David Ray was running, but the flattened cans kept slipping, and a few of them fell. He stopped to pick them up.
Garrett groaned to himself. He couldn't decide if he should
run to David Ray and help him, or just run—as fast and

as far as he could. David Ray stooped down one last time, and Jack Tramp came into the open.

"Hey, you boy! You no-good thief!" The old man was walking fast, his coat hanging open. He was puffing. And there was his gun, waving with every step. "Don't you get away, dammit! Don't you run!" The wheeze of his breathing was louder than his words.

David Ray took one long, slow step toward Garrett.

"You stop, now!" Jack shouted. "Right there! I say stop!"

David Ray's face was white as new paper. Even his freckles were pale. He took another step.

"Hey! Stop!" Then the old man began to run and he stumbled, his arms flying cockeyed. The gun roared.

Garrett's ears rang so with the blast that he nearly missed the cry of pain, long and high and terrible, that came with it. Then everything was quiet and the fear struck him, hard as a bullet. Linnie. He had forgotten Linnie.

Garrett could see Jack Tramp sitting awkwardly on the ground, and David Ray standing still as a tree with all the shiny cans at his feet like fallen leaves. He couldn't make himself look around. His neck was stiff as an iron pipe, his coat collar choked him. He didn't want to know: he had to know.

Then David Ray found his voice, which was shaky at first but got stronger with every word. "Look at that, old Jack Tramp, or whatever your name is—just look at that!" David put one hand on his hip and pointed with the other, accusingly. "You went and shot a poor innocent old dog!"

Linnie! Garrett got himself turned around. There, in the middle of the lane, was Jefferson, strung out like one of

the frost-killed tomato vines in Jack's garden. The dog had bright blood showing, but he wasn't dead; his sides heaved up and down.

Garrett ran around the corner of Mr. Murdock's back lot toward the wagon with his heart thumping against his ribs. She wasn't in the wagon, he could see that. He began to pull at the tall weeds, expecting to find her crumpled on the ground. He had left her with the dog, hadn't he?

"Boo!" she said from under the wagon. "I fooled you, didn't I?" She came crawling out, her red hat flopping over one eye. "I don't like it here," she said, tuning into a whine. "That old dog, he ran off from me. And I heard a lot of yelling and a big loud bang—Garrett, let's go home."

Garrett held his stomach. "Why do you do it?" he demanded, and he knew his voice was fierce. "Why do you hide from people all the time? It's really dumb." His voice rose up away from him, out of his control. "You shouldn't do it, Linnie! It's stupid!"

She cried because he was shouting at her, and that's how Granpop found them when he came to see what the fuss was about: Garrett with a pale gray face, frightened and angry; Linnie with red eyes and fiery cheeks, wailing.

CHAPTER 8

"What would your father think?" In all the fussing and scolding, Aunt Em's question was the worst because Garrett didn't know the answer and he couldn't put it out of his mind.

Mom's chin shook when she talked to him. "I don't care if it is true that Jack would have given his stuff to the scrap drive anyway—you had no business over there, and you know it! And with Linnie—" She folded her arms, hugging herself as if she were freezing. To Garrett the kitchen seemed too warm, too close. "From now to Christmas," Mom said, "you aren't to set foot off McKay property except for school and special errands."

Christmas! Afterward Garrett thought it wasn't fair. David Ray's punishment was to have his bicycle locked away for six months, but he never rode it in the wintertime anyway.

Beanie and Clarence took it hard about Jefferson, who was sent to a veterinarian in Springtown and never came home. It was funny, Garrett thought, how much the dog mattered to them now. While he lived, Jefferson had roamed the town for food and drunk out of corner puddles when his own dish was empty, which was often. Once Beanie had helped Stanley tie a match to Jefferson's tail and they had lit it, just to see what would happen. What happened was that Jefferson sat right down on it, yowling like a cat, and snuffed it out. David Ray had watched and told Garrett all about it.

Now Beanie would sit on the lumber stack in the school-yard and say, "He was a good old dog, wasn't he? Wasn't he a good old dog?" over and over. Clarence called Jack Tramp every name he knew, including two that Garrett had never heard before, ones that weren't even written by the towel box in the boys' toilet. And Clarence was think-ing a lot more than he said, Garrett could tell from his eyes.

For a day or two in Merrittsburg there was as much talk about Jack Tramp as there was about the war and the weather. Paul Darcy told the old man that he needed a gun just like his for a collection he was going to start, and offered to pay a price so far above its worth that Jack agreed. It was common knowledge in town that the post-master had no interest in guns at all, and that he didn't have extra money for buying them at inflated prices, either. Clarence and Beanie's father brought an empty cigar box for the candy counter at the Post Office and insisted that Mr. Darcy keep it there until he had enough contributions to pay himself back.

"You did us a big favor, Darcy, all of us," said Mr. Grant. "Everybody's willing to chip in a little." Garrett was struggling with the combination lock on Granpop's mailbox; it was much harder to work the number when you were concentrating on someone else's conversation at the same time.

"No telling what he might have hit next time with that thing—or who." Mr. Grant's wide neck rose out of his work jacket like a smokestack above a factory. He was a huge man, with a temper to match his size. Garrett was nervous just being near him. He kept remembering things:

the marks on Clarence's back after Jack's window was broken, and the way he had once seen Mr. Grant and his wife on their front porch shouting right into each other's faces.

Mr. Darcy glanced at Garrett, who was slipping toward the door. "I did what seemed was best, that's all," he said to Mr. Grant. "It was the only way I could think of to part him from that thing—he needs money plain enough." Mr. Darcy reached out and caught Garrett's hand as he went by, pressing into his palm two candies, hard brown butterscotch, without missing a word. "Age is gettin' the best of him, y'know? And we'll all be old one day, you have to remember that." He laughed. "Some of us sooner than others."

Mr. Grant paid for a small can of tobacco, making the coins go *thunk* against the counter. "Huh!" he said. Garrett waved his thanks to the postmaster and let himself out the door as Mr. Grant talked on. "God knows, if I ever do get that senseless, I hope someone has me put away, and that's the truth."

Later that evening David Ray's mother came to talk to Garrett's mother. They shut themselves in the living room, but since Aunt Em had gone home and Granpop was in the cellar tinkering with the furnace, both Garrett and Linnie sat close to the door, where they could hear.

"Our kids are all we've got left, Jane—you know that!" Mrs. Allen's voice was urgent and high-pitched; Garrett imagined how her bright, tight curls would be bobbing as she talked, her eyes snapping like David Ray's. As far as Garrett knew, there wasn't any Mr. Allen. Some people said he had gone off to California with another woman and others said he was making corn liquor back in the mountains and getting rich. Probably, Garrett reasoned, he had died a long time ago because David Ray acted as if he had never known such a person.

"We can't take a chance it will happen again, can we?" Mrs. Allen's voice was loud, then softer, then loud again. She was walking around the room, Garrett supposed, judging from the way her voice kept changing. His own mother seemed calmer, seemed to be sitting still. "Maybe the gun did go off accidentally, like he says," Mrs. Allen went on. "But the dog's just as dead, and you know as well as I do that it's only by the grace of God it wasn't one of our boys."

"Or Linnie." Garrett heard the relief, still there in his mother's voice after more than two days. "I get the shakes just thinking about her over there in that wagon. But, Iris—" she paused and talked more softly, so that Garrett could barely hear what she said. "I look at it this way. The boys shouldn't have been there in the first place; and in the second place, Jack doesn't have his gun any more. So I don't see what there's left to do about it."

David Ray's mother talked for a long time, too low for Garrett to hear. He grew almost drowsy as he listened, lulled by the drone of their voices. Then suddenly Mrs. Allen's tone was sharp: "He ought to be put out at the County Farm where someone can watch him every minute, that's what I think!" She came bursting out the door so fast that Garrett was nearly knocked over.

"Well, hi!" she said to him, grinning David Ray's same grin. It was easy for Garrett to see why David Ray loved her so much that he even bragged about her cooking, although mostly what she cooked was soup beans. Garrett thought that Mrs. Allen was the prettiest woman in Merrittsburg. He had said as much to Aunt Em once, but his aunt had only sniffed. "Bleaches her hair," Aunt Em had said shortly. "She's a pepperpot." Whatever that meant.

"You all ready for Halloween, Garrett?" Mrs. Allen asked him. "David's looking for you to go trick or treat with him tomorrow night."

Garrett opened his mouth to say "sure thing," but he heard his mother's voice instead of his own. "He's not going this year, Iris. Too many tricks already."

"But, Mom—" He had never supposed that staying on McKay property meant staying there on Beggars' Night, too.

"But nothing," his mother said firmly, with a tight face. She held the door open for David Ray's mother, and after she had shut it, stood looking out into the night with her head against the glass. Garrett knew it was no use to argue.

On Beggars' Night, two pirates knocked on the door, as well as a witch, a rabbit, and assorted ghosts. Linnie kept telling Garrett how wonderful it was that he was staying home to help her pass out the apples.

"Next year I'll be big, and we'll both go—okay? You won't have to stay in any more, and we'll both go."

"Okay, okay." Garrett kept agreeing with her just to make her be quiet. She was a brat, rubbing it in like that— just like Stanley's sister who had the desk behind him at school and kept whispering, "You shouldn't *do* that, Garrett," if he so much as blinked his eyes.

He watched for David Ray and Stanley and the Grant brothers, but they didn't come. Maybe they had been warned to stay away from Jack Tramp's end of town. He pictured them on the road behind the cemetery now, stuffing themselves with popcorn and molasses candy. If it wasn't for that old Nazi, Garrett thought, he'd be right there with them, having the moonlight shivers and a glorious time.

If it wasn't for all those other Nazis, he thought, his father would be here too, passing out the apples. One year Andy McKay had dressed in old clothes and the most terrifying mask that Garrett had ever seen, and when the beggars came knocking he had jumped right out the door into their midst. The brave ones who didn't run had been rewarded with two apples.

"That's a long face you've got," Granpop said.

"I'm tired, I guess," lied Garrett. He was glad when it was time to go to bed, where he could pull the covers up around his ears and be done with the sound of Linnie's voice, at least.

But she was excited, chattering long after she'd been tucked in. "Trick or treat, Stuffed Mabel, trick or treat! Now you say it, Mabel. *Trick or treat! Trick or treat!*"

"Be quiet, can't you?" He was beginning to feel sleepy, watching the maple tree shadows that danced like goblins on the far wall. The wind was up, and leaf-witches sailed between the moon and the window shade.

"Garrett, let me sit on your bed and look out—please?"

He answered with a grumble, but he flopped over on one side and drew up his knees to make room.

"Don't let the shade go clear to the top," he said from a corner of the pillow.

"I won't." She pulled the shade out from the bottom of the window, edges scraping the curtains, stuck her head under and pulled the rag doll up beside her. "Lookit,

Stuffed Mabel! Jack Tramp's having Halloween! See his pumpkin face, Mabel? It's *ugly*! Look at that old crooked mouth—"

"Pipe down!" Garrett kicked her, but not too hard. If she got hurt she'd go tattle. "You and your dumb fairy tales," he muttered.

She was getting ready to cry—he sensed it—when Mom came up the stairs and into her room. The bedsprings squeaked when she sat down, and her shoes thumped the floor gently, one and then the other, as she kicked them off.

"You better get in your own bed," Garrett said under his breath. When Linnie moved, he stretched his legs full length. Out of habit, he said a silent good-night to his father, and then he went to sleep.

Bombs were dropping from a plane with a pirate at the controls. He had an eye patch that covered his whole face, but somehow Garrett knew that it was Mr. Grant. And a gypsy lady with a bag of popcorn balls screamed above the pounding—*thwack*, shriek, *whump*, shriek—in a crazy rhythm.

With effort Garrett fought clear of the dream. He sat up in bed, confused. He was awake, he was sure. But the pounding went on. And the shouting.

"Wa-ake up in there! Get up! Leee-o! Jane!"

Garrett fumbled for his jeans and his shoes and stumbled past his mother's room. She was up and gone. He hurried down toward the light that showed at the bottom of the stairs.

Granpop was just letting Aunt Em in at the kitchen door, and she was gulping for breath like a new-caught fish. Her old corduroy wrapper was fastened crooked, her gray braids undone. She beckoned them with both hands.

"Come quick!" she managed to say. "Bring the buckets, and the gunny sacks!"

"Em!" Mom was flinging a coat over her pajamas. "Dear God! What's burning?"

"Old Jack's house—with him in it, likely. I saw it out the window as I was getting to bed. Hurry, now!"

Aunt Em ran out into the night, with Granpop and Mom behind her. Garrett thought they didn't even know he was up, but over his shoulder Granpop called for him to bring the broom, and Mom shouted, "Bring both of them!" He pulled the two straw brooms from the corner by the waste can and ran after them. By the time he reached the lane, the dark wind had turned him stiff with cold; then the leaping flames on Jack Tramp's rickety door-steps began to warm him.

Aunt Em rapped on Jack's side window, calling him, banging as hard as she could while the fire rose up around his doorway at the front.

"Don't go to the door!" she screamed. "Come out the window! Jack! Jack! Adolf Schilling, get out here! Come on to the window!"

Granpop wet the old sacks he'd brought with water from Jack's barrel and beat at the flames while Mom used the side of one broom to smack at the spreading edges of the fire. Garrett stood numb, staring. The steps had now fallen clear away and some of the siding boards were be-ginning to burn. The wood box and everything in it was gone, and the metal junk box glowed like a winter stove. Jack Tramp was caught in his little house. He was going to burn up sure as if he'd been bombed. Garrett had been to the movies twice last summer, and he remembered the newsreels.

"Hey!" Granpop shouted at him. "Don't lean on that broom, boy—use it!"

Garrett began to flail at the sparks popping among the

leaves. There was not a lot of smoke, but what there was made him cough, made his eyes burn. Jack Tramp must be choking, he thought.

At that moment Aunt Em's banging stopped. The old man came to his window, forced it open, and wriggled out. He landed heavily on his left side, but he sat up quickly, his breath rasping like a file on dry wood.

"You all right?" demanded Aunt Em, herself panting.

He blinked and began to rub his head. Then he peered up at her in the wicked, dancing light. "What you in your night clothes for, old woman?"

Aunt Em clutched her wrapper. "Your house is afire!" she shouted.

"Huh? Huh?" For a long time he seemed not to understand. His eyes were cast over like a foggy day, so that Garrett couldn't tell even by looking straight at him if he knew what was happening. But whether the old man knew it or not, Granpop and Mom put out the fire, with Garrett and Aunt Em helping. Then Mr. Murdock came hurrying through the weeds with an extra bucket, but by that time there was only the moonlight to see by.

"Ruined your door," Granpop said wearily to Jack. "Made a hole clean through the wall, too." He was puffing.

Mr. Murdock examined the damage, nodding in an official way. He worked at the Springtown courthouse, and his authority was as easy to see as his mustache.

"You can't stay here," he said to Jack Tramp.

"Can too," said Jack. "My own place, ain't it?"

"Good Lord, man, be reasonable. There's a hole big enough for a bear to walk through."

Jack Tramp threw back his head and laughed. "Shows

what you know," he said triumphantly. "No bears around here!"

For a moment, for one breath of time, Garrett liked the old man. Thataway to tell him, he thought. And then he remembered everything that the fire had melted out of his mind, and he was suddenly very cold. His arms hurt. He began to shiver with such force that his teeth rattled, and Aunt Em looked around at him.

"Look at you!" she cried. "Just your pajama top—you'll be sick."

Garrett's mother touched his arm. "Come on home," she said, "and we'll fix some sandwiches. Come on, Em. You too, Mr. Murdock. And you, Jack, you'd better come over and stay."

Mr. Murdock shook his head. "I have to be getting back to bed," he said. "Thank you, of course. But I have to be at work early, you know. Jack can come to my house for the night, until he gets a chance to look things over and decide what to do."

"Won't need to do that," said Jack Tramp. Without a thank-you or a good-night he disappeared into his garage and didn't come back out.

"He's a case," said Mr. Murdock, yawning. "He's definitely a case. Someone will have to do something about him."

Mr. Murdock went up the lane toward his own house, and the McKays crossed the road in weary silence, dragging the blackened brooms and a few of the sacks, still heavy with water. By the well curb, Granpop stopped. "Do you suppose Linnie slept through all this?"

It was Garrett who ran ahead to see, and for once he

found Linnie right where she belonged. She was uncovered, with one foot dangling over the edge and her head on Stuffed Mabel's backside. But she was sleeping without a twitch, safely accounted for.

Garrett looked at her and wished suddenly and painfully that his Dad could know. He wanted his father to know that he, Garrett, had been in the heat of the trouble and not tucked away safe at home like Linnie, like a baby. "See?" he whispered, and he tiptoed out of the room.

There was a long session at the bathroom sink, each of them taking a turn to clean their sooty hands and arms and faces. The smell of pine soap, strong as it was, failed to cover the smell of charred wood and burned trash that clung to their hair and their clothing. Garrett was so tired that he scrubbed his right elbow twice and forgot the left one, but he was revived somewhat by the toast and cheese and cider that Mom and Aunt Em set out. The four of them sat down to eat and warm themselves and talk about the fire.

"Pure meanness is what it was," Aunt Em said decisively. "One of those boys from out beyond the cemetery, or somewhere, you mark my word. Just naturally came down here and set that old man's house afire." She got up to make herself a cup of tea. "It's a crime, that's what it is."

Granpop shook his head. "We can't say that, Em. We don't know, and there's no way for us to tell, and old Jack—he doesn't know what happened, that's sure." He closed his eyes for a moment, and Garrett saw how the little wrinkles in his eyelids were still dark with ash. "It may be just his years tellin' on him. All that junk he always keeps by the door, y'know—it wouldn't take more than one match tossed out, or one old cigar stump, and bing!

there she starts. He's not careful the way he used to be—
he forgets things."

Garrett's mother pushed her plate away, as if she had
grown too tired to eat. "There's more danger that he'll
hurt himself than anyone else, you know that?" she said. "I
suppose Mr. Murdock's right. Somebody will have to do
something about him."

Do something, do something, do something. The words
made a senseless refrain in Garrett's head; his eyes kept
losing focus. The next day Aunt Em told him he had fallen
asleep with his head on the kitchen table and Granpop had
helped him upstairs to bed. But Garrett didn't remember.

CHAPTER 10

Jack Tramp nailed three wide boards across the hole in his house, and went on living in his garage. "He'll freeze in there," Aunt Em said when the weather turned rainy. "How does he cook or anything? Tell me that." But the old man turned away all offers of help.

At school, Garrett spent most of his free time answering questions about the fire.

"How do you think it started?" David Ray demanded, still eager after they'd talked about it a dozen times. "Huh, Garrett? What do you really think?"

"Nobody knows," Garrett said patiently, facing most of the regular crowd at the lumber stack. "Maybe it was a cigar he tossed in his trash can, or a match or something. He doesn't know himself, I don't think." Garrett shrugged. "My Aunt Em thinks someone might have set his house on fire for a Halloween trick. She says not too many years ago someone turned over his outhouse for a joke."

"Some joke," said Stanley appreciatively. "Geez, I bet that stunk!"

"Yeah, but listen," David Ray said soberly, "that's different than a fire. I mean, who would set a fire? Just imagine, burning up, how it must be—your skin and all.

Does it get all black and wrinkly, do you suppose? The Germans do it to people, you know it? It happens in the war all the time.'"

Garrett glared at him. "Why don't you just shut up?"

"Oh—" David Ray dropped his eyes. "I forgot," he said.

Stanley broke in to say that it would have served Jack Tramp right if his house had burned clear down to the ground, and Beanie agreed with him. Completely and absolutely, so he said. After all, Jack was probably a German spy. Maybe he'd been trying to destroy some evidence or something, and that's how the fire had started. David Ray picked up this suggestion and began to concoct a story about it, making it all sound very convincing. Garrett only half listened. He was wondering what Clarence thought, but Clarence had not been to school for several days. He had eaten too much of something on Beggars' Night, Beanie said, and had been sick at his stomach ever since.

On the following Saturday, Beanie and Stanley and David Ray appeared in Granpop's pasture just before noon, with Beanie's old football, a prize won from a trash bin during the first scrap drive of the year. Clarence, looking a bit pale, was with them. "Want to have a game?" he asked when Garrett came to greet them. Garrett was flattered; now that he wasn't allowed to go anywhere, they had come to him. Of course he wanted to have a game.

It was only natural, he supposed, that the boys should seem as interested in staring at Jack Tramp's house as they were in football. The sides—three against two—weren't even, and then it was hard to run because the field was soft and slippery underfoot, mucky as chocolate pudding. The day was unpleasant, the clouds dark and heavy. It was going to rain again. If things got any wetter, Garrett thought, Mr. Darcy would start talking about Noah and the Ark whenever anyone went for the mail. Even Granpop said the ground had soaked up as much as it could hold; two more drops and there'd be high water.

"Linnie, move!" shouted one of the boys. She had wandered into the pasture and sat down right on the rock they were using to mark the goal line.

For answer she stuck out her chin and bent over her doll. "Aren't they mean, Mabel? We don't like boys, do we?"

"You'll get hurt, Linnie," called David Ray. "One of us great big football players might squash you."

She giggled; she liked David Ray. Once, to Garrett's disgust, she had told David she was going to marry him when she grew up.

"You're getting all muddy," Garrett said. "You know what Aunt Em will say."

Linnie turned and glared at him. "I'm watching the man!" she shouted, as if that explained everything.

"What man?" Stanley, who was closest, went over beside her, then hooked one arm above his head as a signal for the rest to join him.

"Who is that guy, anyway?" asked Beanie.

From Linnie's rock they all could see a man in the small doorway of Jack Tramp's garage, leaning in, talking, waving one hand to emphasize his words.

"He's from the County," Stanley guessed. "See that car in the lane with the special tag on it?"

"I bet he takes the old buzzard away," said Beanie. "About time, too."

Stanley nodded. "Good riddance," he agreed.

Garrett tried, without success, to imagine Jack's house

standing empty, his garden unplanted, his yard grown over. The stranger walked away from the garage, coming slowly toward the road. He spent a long time looking at the burned-out spot at the front of Jack's house, and poked with his toe in the little heap of rubble where the steps had been.

"He's awful fat," said Linnie in her high, clear voice. Beanie began to giggle, and the stranger looked their way. It was true that his brown suit coat was strained across a very wide middle, but he had an ordinary, pleasant face, rather like someone's uncle. Smiling, he waved at the children and began to walk toward them.

"Oh, brother," said Clarence. Garrett hunched his shoulders. Out of the leaden sky fell one slow sprinkle and then another.

"Maybe you kids can help me out," the round man said, ignoring the rain. He leaned across the wire fence that kept the McKays' cow from straying into the road, and took from his breast pocket a small notebook. "Mr. Carter's my name, and I work for County Welfare." He waited while they nodded hello. "You all know Mr. Schilling over there, I suppose."

They all nodded again, even Linnie, although she moved behind Garrett and poked his leg. "Is that Jack Tramp?" she whispered anxiously. "Is that who?"

"We've had reports," said Mr. Carter, "that he's been threatening neighborhood children, and using abusive language, and generally not behaving very well." He smiled. "That's right, isn't it? And he discharged a gun on one occasion, at least—is that so?"

David Ray stepped forward. "Boy, sir, you said it!" he began proudly. "That old man come out of his house a-swingin' that old gun, and there I stood. All I wanted to do was collect his things for the scrap drive so he wouldn't have to bother with them himself, and—"

"Yes, I see," said the man from the County, breaking David Ray's story in mid-sentence. "You must be the Allen boy, then. I've talked to your mother already. Now, about this fire—did any of you see it? He tells me someone tried to burn him out." Mr. Carter shook his head. "Uptown here they tell me he likely started it himself with his cigar—careless, you know." He bent toward them. "Now see, kids, if he's a danger to himself and other people, we'll have to do something, that's all. What we care about is everybody being safe—you understand that? And I just happen to think that kids know a lot their parents don't, sometimes." He began to look at each of them in turn. "So what about this fire?"

Garrett licked his upper lip so as to be ready to speak when the older eyes met his. But another voice came first.

"His jack-o'-lantern burned up, prob'ly," Linnie said, coming closer to the fence. Garrett blinked. Linnie was more likely to run from strangers than talk to them. Right now she would be hiding, he felt certain, if David Ray had not already spoken.

"The wind went *whoosh*, all spooky," continued Linnie, "and he had a pumpkin face on top of his trash can—I saw from the window." There was a murmur among the boys and a soft "uh-huh" from the man across the fence.

He smiled at Linnie in an encouraging way. "You live here?" he asked, pointing to the McKay house. Linnie nodded solemnly, and the man rubbed his chin. "What else, little one?" he prompted.

"That's all," said Linnie, "except it was a funny pumpkin. Just a big mouth, real crooked—you know, like a Hitler thing." She raised her arm and drew the shape of a swastika in the air.

Garrett tried to breathe and couldn't. Linnie was telling the absolute truth, he knew it. And he should have guessed. Or they should have told him. Which one of them had carved Jack's pumpkin? he wondered.

Mr. Carter was studying Linnie. "Could you tell me all that just one more time?" he coaxed, beckoning her closer, away from the others. "Just so I'd have it straight, okay?"

Linnie adjusted her grip on Stuffed Mabel's leg and smiled happily. "I'm too little to go trick or treat," she said. "But I have a witch's hat." She was getting warmed up for a long story, Garrett could tell. She was going to talk a blue streak. Maybe he ought to go get Mom or Granpop. While he tried to decide what to do, he felt a tug on his shirt.

"Sssssst! Come here." Clarence pulled Garrett back from the rest of the boys, who were edging toward Linnie. "Let's you and me set up the next play," he suggested loudly, crouching down to Garrett's height. "You better tell that guy how your little sister makes up stories," he said in Garrett's ear.

All at once Garrett understood. He thought of Jack Tramp's broken window and of Jefferson lying in the lane. He knew. "It was you," he hissed.

"Yeah, but nobody else knows about it." Clarence's eyes were pleading. "I never meant to set a fire," he whispered urgently. "I never would do that, you know I wouldn't. I just wanted to show him what we thought of him. He was supposed to come out and see the thing, for cripe's sake, not sit around and let it catch his house on fire!"

Garrett's feelings twisted themselves into a knot like a

giant pretzel. Linnie was telling the absolute truth, and so was Clarence: Clarence would throw mud balls into Jack Tramp's water barrel, but he wouldn't set his house on fire, not on purpose. Still, if Mr. Grant found out what had happened—Garrett felt a tremor of sympathy. No one would punish Linnie, no matter what. It was Clarence who needed him, was practically begging. Garrett was filled with a sudden feeling of fierce loyalty. Something fluttered in his throat; it was the way he felt when the high school band played "The Star Spangled Banner."

"Okay," he said under his breath, and pushed his way to the fence. "Hey, Linnie," he said, interrupting. "It's starting to rain. You'd better go home." And to the man across the fence he said, "That's my little sister, and I'm sorry if she bothered you. She tells big lies all the time like that—it's the way she plays, pretending." And that was so, Garrett assured himself: she did tell stories, she did pretend. But the truth of his words did nothing to sweeten their taste. This was different. He knew it. And so did Linnie.

The man straightened up, frowning, and Beanie began to snicker. "Know what?" he said. "She talks to that rag doll and then she holds it up to her ear so it can answer back."

"But I did too see a pumpkin!" protested Linnie. "It was real! I saw it!"

David Ray nodded and grinned, almost fondly. "Mister," he said, "she's got *some* imagination. I almost believed there was a pumpkin, myself."

"There was!" She began to cry. "Honest there was!"

Sighing, the man tucked his notebook inside his coat. He looked hard at Garrett. "You never saw any jack-o'-lantern with a swastika on it, or anything like that?"

"No, sir," Garrett replied. "Never. I swear." Relief fell on him like the cold, fine drops of rain. He hadn't seen it. He crossed his fingers behind his back. "She made it all up, I guess."

Linnie's face had lost its color. She grabbed at Garrett's coat sleeve. "You never looked," she said. "You didn't."

The man from the County had turned away. "Thanks," he said over his shoulder. "Things have gone so far now I suppose that part doesn't matter too much anyway. Be seeing you kids." He squeezed behind the wheel of his black coupe, lifted his hand in salute, and drove away.

"Hey, Linnie—" Garrett looked down to tell her it was all right, to explain that he really believed her, but she had slipped away. "Where'd she go?" he demanded. He turned around to scan the pasture and the barn lot and the yard, but he couldn't see Linnie.

Across the road, a rough voice called. "Boy! Hey there, boy!" And Jack Tramp came out of his garage and shuffled toward them.

Clarence edged away. "I have to get home," he said, beginning to run. "Come on, Beanie." Beanie scooped up the football and loped after his brother, with Stanley following. David Ray looked once at Jack Tramp and once at the three runners. "See you later," he said to Garrett, and hurried to join them.

"Hey, boy!" shouted Jack again. As he came closer his voice seemed louder and louder. "You talk to that fella? What'd he want, huh?" The old man coughed and spat into the mud; he kept one fist pressed against the middle of his chest as he talked.

Garrett looked over his shoulder, both ways, wishing that someone would call him away, would rescue him.

"Snoopin', wasn't he?" pressed the old man, who was now unbearably close, blowing his sour breath in Garrett's face with every word. "Wants me to sign a paper—you know that? Know what for?" Jack stopped to cough. "Wants me to go to the County Farm! Hah!" He leaned across the fence and shook one finger at Garrett. "Won't do it, boy. No, sir. I knew me an old fella once, had to live there." His pale eyes fixed themselves on a point beyond Garrett, far away, and he lowered his voice. "They got funny people there, you know that? Old women and everything—he told me. Set in their chairs all day and rock, just rock. I got me a good place here, boy, just look at it— nothin' wrong with that garage. That snoopin' fella says I can't stay in it, though. Gotta move. Huh. Comin' back in the morning, he says. Bring his truck maybe. Get my things." Trembling, the old man began to rock his body to and fro. "Won't go to that place. Won't. Just won't."

The boy couldn't bear to look at him. He moved backward, then turned and ran for the house, splattering through the long wet grass.

CHAPTER 11

Garrett burst into the kitchen, slammed the door, and leaned against it as if he had just made a great escape. Granpop stood silent by the sink, just watching him. Why didn't he say something? Garrett wondered. Mom and Aunt Em came from the dining room, one behind the other like runners in a race. Each of them, he supposed, wanted the honor of being first to remind him that he was too old to be slamming doors and tracking mud on the linoleum. But no one said a word. The three adults kept looking at each other and then at Garrett. Finally Granpop cleared his throat, and Mom broke into a smile that crinkled up her face like tissue paper around a gift. Sudden hope rose up in Garrett like a kite in a puff of wind; he had the dizzy sensation of height.

"Tell him!" commanded Aunt Em. "Tell him right now!"

Garrett's mother reached out and hugged him so hard that, big as he was, his muddy feet came clear up off the floor. "He's alive!" she cried. "Your dad's alive! We just got a phone call."

"From *Dad*?"

"No—"

"Who from, then? How do they know? Where is he? Is he all right?" The questions came bubbling up out of Garrett, and he hiccuped because his mother was still squeezing him.

"Red Cross," Granpop explained. "Have to get the details later. All they could tell us was that he's with his unit, so he's not a prisoner—we know that much."

"Is he hurt, Mom?"

For a moment she tightened her arms around his shoulders. "He's *alive*," she said.

"Oh, boy!" Garrett said, pulling away from her. "Oh boy, wow!"

"It's wonderful," declared Aunt Em. "It's the grandest thing I ever heard." Then she plopped down in her wicker chair to celebrate in privacy, with her apron over her head.

Garrett clomped his feet, trying to dance a jig. "I have to go tell the guys—okay? Is it okay if I go find them? I'll come right back, I promise—okay?"

His mother nodded, and he bounded out into the wet, dull world from which he had just come. In his eyes everything was changed, turned from gray to silver, beautiful. The encounter with Jack Tramp and the County Welfare man seemed a long-ago thing, dim and unimportant. He had room for only one concern, and that was the news singing inside him.

Garrett ran as far as the cross street before he found anyone to tell. It was only Arnold Anderson, who stared and picked his nose and didn't say anything; he was too shy to talk to older boys. Disgusted, Garrett ran on to David Ray's house and, since David wasn't there, panted out his news to Mrs. Allen. Afterward, after Mrs. Allen had cried a little and hugged him just the way his mother had done, he found Beanie. Beanie had to hear the news twice before he would believe it, and then he went on with Garrett to the grocery store and to the Post Office. Garrett wanted to go knocking on every door in Merrittsburg and say, "Guess what? They found my dad!"

But he had already stayed away too long. It was raining steadily now, and Garrett's jacket was wet enough to dampen his shirt. He was getting cold, he was hungry. "You tell the other guys," he instructed Beanie, and he ran for home.

Aunt Em was there to meet him at the door, and between her eyes were three pinches of skin like the folds of a tiny fan. "Is she with you?"

"Who?"

"Linnie. We can't find her."

Linnie. He let out his breath slowly, hissing air the way Beanie's old football did under a tackle. He began to remember Clarence's eyes, pleading; Linnie's eyes, betrayed. He felt himself grow hot with shame.

"She's behind the door, probably," he said, hoping—praying—that it was true.

Aunt Em shook her head with irritation. "No, she's not. Don't you think I know enough to look there?"

Garrett chewed the inside of his cheek. "She goes to the barn a lot."

"Leo went through every crack and cranny out there."

"The chicken house?" Linnie was afraid of the rooster, who was old and vile-tempered and had once mistaken her bare toe for chicken feed. Only by a miracle would she be at the chicken house.

"Not there either," Aunt Em said. "I looked myself."

"She's gone over to Mrs. Tanner's!" exclaimed Garrett with sudden inspiration, remembering how Linnie liked to play with the china cats that lined the widow's cupboard. "I'll bet anything."

Aunt Em puckered up her mouth for sour apples. "Don't bet something you want to keep, then. Your mother just looked over there—nothing. So she and Leo started out in the car, just before you came."

"Well, where could she be?"

"Who knows, child?" Fear came up in Aunt Em's eyes and showed itself before she could blink it away. "Out along the highway maybe, halfway to Springtown, carried off somewhere, drowned in the creek—it makes me sick to think. And today of all days."

"Don't worry, Aunt Em. She's probably just around somewhere, like always." Garrett searched for words to reassure himself. "Remember the time she hid in the cellar behind the pickle crocks and we didn't find her for two hours? And that other time when she got under the hydrangea bushes and went to sleep and never heard us call?"

Aunt Em nodded, but the wrinkles stayed tight between her eyes.

"I'll go find her," Garrett said. "Remember, I found her those other times." Shivering, he took off his wet jacket and bundled himself into Granpop's mackinaw. It was far too big and painfully heavy, but he thought it would keep him dry for a good long time.

Aunt Em gave him a bread-and-butter sandwich and a worried look. "I'll go over the house again," she said, "and mind you be home before dark or we'll have to get the sheriff out for the both of you."

As soon as he stepped outside he saw that the clouds were lower, the rain colder, as if both night and winter were trying to arrive ahead of schedule.

"You'll catch your death," Aunt Em said from the doorway. "You better not go."

Garrett pretended not to hear; he had to go. "I'll be back just as soon as I can," he promised, and he started across the back yard toward the orchard.

If Linnie was outside, he reasoned, she would have looked for some sort of shelter. Behind the apple trees was a berry thicket where early last spring the boys had built a fort of dead branches. They had meant to use it all summer, but then they had discovered, too late, poison ivy growing along the trench they had dug for a latrine. Stanley got itching blisters on his behind, and they had abandoned the fort. But it was a place that Linnie knew about and Garrett thought she might be there: he had a feeling.

He slogged through the tall grass, remembering how his father had told him to look after Linnie. He would find her —he had to—and try to explain about Jack Tramp and Clarence and the pumpkin. Everything was going to be all right; he whistled a bit to prove it.

But the fort in the berry thicket was dripping wet, and empty. It concealed nothing but a few sparrow feathers to mark the spot where one of the barn cats had feasted.

"Linnie! Liiiiin-neeeee!" His voice rose an octave above its normal pitch. "Come on out! I've got something for you!" He didn't know what he could give her; he would think of something. But where was she? What a brat, he thought, trying to cover his desperation with anger. Why did she have to run off like that, anyway?

Garrett sloshed through the barn lot and the chicken

yard, double-checked the woodshed, made a second trip around the barn and then climbed, shakily, into the loft. The hay made him sneeze.

"Liiiiin-neeeee!"

He poked every lump where she might be hiding, but no hat with red pompons appeared. Then he clomped toward the ladder and rattled it as if he had given up and was going away. Holding his breath, he waited for her to stir. Maybe he would hear her talking to Stuffed Mabel. But all he heard was rain on the metal roof, popping like corn in the pan. She wasn't in the barn.

Garrett crouched under the line of the eaves, giving himself another moment of warmth to fight the knots in his stomach. Through a wide crack in the siding he looked down across the bottom field with its straggling November cornstalks. Granpop had hired George Fisher to help him with the harvest, and now the field was bare except for the leavings. Most of the trees along Elm Creek were bare, too, except for the oaks. Garrett could see how high the water was, how uncommonly fast the current ran. He caught his breath, and the inside of his mouth went dry as the hay. What if Linnie had gone to the Stones?

CHAPTER 12

She wouldn't do it, he kept telling himself. She had never gone that far alone. Garrett came down the loft ladder with a peculiar numbness in his knees. She just wouldn't do it, that was all. Mechanically his feet moved down the slope toward the field. She wouldn't; she'd be afraid. He picked his way through the cornfield, where every row of stubble marked the edge of a deepening puddle. He wished he had remembered his boots. He wished it would stop raining.

"Liiiiiiin-neeeeee!" He stopped. It was stupid to go all the way to the Stones, ankle-deep in mud. Linnie wouldn't be there. His shoulders bent under the weight of Granpop's huge, damp coat. But what if she was? What if she had taken Stuffed Mabel to visit her grandmother, or some dumb thing like that?

"Liiiiiin-neeee!" He went on. The path through the trees was under water by an inch or two in several places; the creek's proper banks had disappeared. The middle of the stream swirled and sucked like water running out of a tub. Whole branches bounced downstream carrying clumps of grass and matted leaves. The creek had turned into a witch's stew, thick and brown and bubbling. In the next gully, water had risen as deep as Garrett's knees; to stay out of it he had to walk the trunk of a dead tree. The old wood glistened with wet, slippery moss.

He could go back, he told himself. Linnie probably wasn't at the Stones at all. Probably she was sitting in the kitchen right this minute with her feet in a blanket, having warm milk and a scolding. Probably. Maybe. He crawled across the log on his hands and knees, an inch at a time. When he reached the other side he realized what a waste of energy it had been. He was already so wet that he might as well have walked through the gully.

Just ahead of him the Stones sat, gray and forbidding, half in and half out of the darkening water. On the up-stream side, the wild creek flung itself against the base, fell back and slithered toward the upland end. Garrett kept his distance, scanning the trees, the bushes, the huge fallen rocks. There was no sign of Linnie's red hat or Stuffed Mabel's orange hair.

Carefully he made his way through the brush, keeping to the high ground at the end of the Stones. Toward the downstream side of the abutment, the water was calmer but deeper. The lower bank was covered, and most of the sunken spots along the side of the Stones had disappeared. Only a few gully ridges stood above the flood, leading from Garrett's feet toward the main stream. The creek had overflowed all the places where Granpop liked to fish and was lapping up toward the picnic stone. Garrett peered along the side of the abutment toward the far end. He saw nothing but brown water, gray stone, dark trees. The rain blurred it all together. But surely Linnie wasn't there. He was so filled with relief that he might have cried.

And then he thought: what if she was here and fell in already and they find her floating like a dead fish under the Springtown bridge? The panic of it made him sick at his stomach, and he screamed her name. "Linnie! Linnie! Linnie!"

"Here!" At first the cry was not much louder than two branches squeaking as they rub together in a storm. Then it grew plainer above the constant angry music of the water. "Get me down! Please get me down!"

Shaking, Garrett searched with his eyes. There nothing to see but the rain; he must have imagined the voice. "Where are you?" he cried, starting toward the picnic stone. "Where are you?" He couldn't think what to do; he began to get cramps in his stomach.

"Linnie! Tell me where you are!" He moved cautiously, testing each step, grasping low branches and brush with his stiff hands. Twice the water reached up to wet the bottom of Granpop's coat. "Linnie!"

Then he heard her crying and knew that she was really there. He followed the sound as best he could, moving as far into the water as he thought he dared. She was somewhere on the Stones, he felt sure, but he could not see her. What if she had got to the top somehow? What if she had her foot wedged between two stones or something? There was a funny, terrible taste on the back of his tongue, a sick taste.

"Where are you, Linnie? Wave your hand or something!" He lost his footing and stumbled backward, catching himself at the last moment by clutching the corner of a fallen stone. When his head jerked, he saw the doll. Stuffed Mabel's bright hair spilled over the corner of the ledge that jutted from the end of the Stones along the line of the creek bank. The main current of the flood rushed by around it.

It was possible to climb from the picnic stone to that ledge, Garrett knew. He had done it once, with strong sunlight and dry footing and his father's hand at his elbow. All the low spots, now, were under water. If he tried to climb around and over the fallen stones to get to Linnie, he might get in over his head. And if she tried to get down to him, she'd go under for sure.

The doll disappeared and Linnie's head slowly took its place: two bright pompons, some dark straggles of wet hair, a face that seemed to have taken the color of the Stones. He couldn't see the rest of her.

"I can't get down." Her voice was thin and shaky, the way it always was when she had cried so long she couldn't cry any more. "I got up," she said, "but I can't get down. It wasn't all wet before. It wasn't all deep and scary."

"You aren't hurt, are you?"

"I scratched my knee and got blood on it." She started to whimper.

"Don't cry, Linnie." He swallowed the sick taste on his tongue; he felt like crying himself. "Don't worry. Hold Stuffed Mabel real tight and keep back against the Stones. Okay?" He wanted to tell her that everything would be all right, that he would climb right up there and carry her down and take her home. But how could he lie like that?

"Let me think a minute," he called to her. The rain had faded into sprinkles, but the daylight too had faded so that the sky and the water and the Stones were all part of the dusk. The level of the water crept upward, bit by bit, toward the place where Linnie was. Garrett clenched and unclenched his fists. Every minute that he spent thinking about what to do was another minute for the creek to rise higher and the sky to get darker.

"Hey, boy!" The rough voice came suddenly, quite close beside him. "I been hearin' you yell—saw Leo out lookin'. What's the matter? She stuck?"

Garrett's knees went weak with surprise as Jack Tramp came out of the trees to his right. The old man was wet to the waist and mud-splattered, with new dirt over old on his tattered winter jacket. Rain had smoothed his hair so that his head was sleek and shining. Garrett had never thought that he would welcome the sight of Jack Tramp, that he would be ready to beg his help, eager for his companionship. Yet here he was, and the boy was so relieved that even his coat felt lighter. Whatever happened, Garrett thought, at least he would not be alone with the darkness and the water.

"I don't know if I can get her down," Garrett said, quietly, so that Linnie wouldn't hear.

The little girl dangled one arm over the side of the ledge; her fingertips touched water. "Stuffed Mabel wants her supper," she said, her voice trembling. "Stuffed Mabel's afraid."

"It's okay," Garrett called out. "We're coming." He looked swiftly at the old man. "Aren't we?"

Jack Tramp frowned, studying the Stones and the water. Garrett in turn studied Jack Tramp, noticing for the first time the bag he carried.

The red mesh sack was stuffed full, bulging across the old man's back like a deformity. There were clothes in the bag, Garrett could see that, and a cup and saucepan with some tableware that gave a clang every time Jack shifted his weight. Jack Tramp must be going away, leaving. The boy stared. Jack Tramp wasn't going to the County Farm after all. The knots in Garrett's stomach grew tighter;

inside Granpop's coat he was too hot and too cold, all at the same time. Linnie began to cry again.

Finally Jack rubbed his nose and grunted. "See that tree?" He pointed. "See how it forks?"

Garrett looked at the spot, a joining of oak limbs some three or four feet from the end of the Stones, and well above Linnie's reach.

"You climb up there," Jack Tramp directed. "I wade in and get up where she is, see? Then I lift her up and you help her into the tree and down. Huh?"

Garrett considered the oak tree, and the blurring in his eyes told him that he couldn't climb it. He swallowed. What other way was there? "Sure," he said. "That's how we'll do it."

The old man settled his bag of belongings on a stump, then splashed along the picnic stone, making his way toward the ledge. The pathway led down before it led up, and there was one awful moment when Jack stumbled and disappeared altogether. He bobbed up, spluttering. "Climb!" shouted the old man. "Come on, boy!"

Garrett climbed. His breathing was as rough in his throat as the bark in his hands, but he climbed. From the top of one angled stone he reached the lowest branch, and after that there were three easy pulls and then one long one that brought him into the fork. He looked down at Linnie, called out, waved his hand.

Jack Tramp was just edging up onto the ledge. What if Linnie was afraid of him, Garrett thought. What if she looked at him and got all excited and fell over the edge? Water ran off the old man's head, dripped out of his sleeves, leaked from under his coat. His breath gurgled. Linnie was going to scream, Garrett thought. Maybe she'd scream so loud that it would scare Jack and then they'd both fall over the edge. But she stared at the newcomer for only a second, and then she scooted over to make room for him.

Garrett glanced below him and was suddenly grateful for the coming dark. He could see the brown oak leaves on the limb where his feet were, but not much else. He could hear the water, he could sense it beneath him, but he could not see it. The place where he would fall, if he fell, was hidden from him. One-handed, he gripped the oak branch with the best of his strength.

"Lift her up!" Garrett called. "I—I'm ready!"

On the stone ledge, the old man shook his head. He was crouched beside Linnie, breathing hard, pressing one hand to his chest. "Can't," he said finally. "Done—somethin'—to myself." He took a slow, noisy breath. "Got a pain, boy. You better go for somebody."

Linnie looked from one to the other. "Please," she begged. "I want to get down. I want to go home." Without warning she scrambled to her feet and reached for Garrett, stretching her body out over the water toward the oak tree. The old man lunged forward and caught her by the waist, drawing her back against the solid wall of the Stones. He sank back on his heels with Linnie safely jailed in his wet lap.

"Aaah," he groaned, and he parted his lips in something like a smile. "You and me, girl, we stay here for a bit, huh? Send your brother, okay?" The old man coughed. "Let him get wet. Not us, huh?" Without looking away from Linnie, he motioned for Garrett to climb down.

Garrett felt as if he had grown fast to the tree. His hands were stiff and shivering, weak; his legs were too heavy to move. Clumsily he groped for the first foothold, as Jack Tramp talked to Linnie.

"Who's this, huh?" He reached for the sopping rag doll and shook it gently. "What's her name, huh? Lena? Always favored that name. Is that it?" His breath came a bit more easily now, his words closer together. "You know about Lena?" The old man cleared his throat and began to sing, his voice grating like Aunt Em's butcher knife against the grindstone: "Lena, my Lena, her last name is Schmiddle, she looks like a featherbed tied in the middle. . . ."

"You silly thing." There was a hint of life in Linnie's voice. "This is Mabel. *Stuffed* Mabel."

Garrett's foot touched the stone beneath the tree; water swirled above his ankles.

"Mabel!" exclaimed Jack, and coughed. "Can she dance?"

Garrett could not see them now. He sloshed away from the Stones, feeling his way.

"Hurry, boy!"

Garrett tried to run, though his clothes were so heavy with water that he could scarcely move. If Jack Tramp can sing, he thought, then I can run. And he ran.

CHAPTER 13

Garrett came out of the trees along the edge of Granpop's bottom field and stopped for a moment, puffing. His shoes were heavy with mud, a punishment for his legs. Far away at the top of the slope—a hundred miles at least, or so it seemed—a prick of light marked the barn door. It would take forever to get to the house. He glanced back toward the rising water, wondering how long it would be before the creek spilled over the top of the ledge.

"Granpop!" he shouted. "Hey, Granpop! Anybody, hey! Help!"

Quiet. He slogged on. Maybe Mom and Granpop were still out on the highway looking for Linnie. Or maybe they had come home and started out again to look for him, too, but in the wrong direction. What if he got to the house and couldn't find anyone but Aunt Em to help? The worrying made him clumsy, and he tripped.

Something bigger than a log had washed along the edge of the cornfield and lay in the wet weeds, blocking his way. When his knee struck it, there was a curious hollow thump. Quickly he examined the thing with his hands. The outline was familiar somehow; his cold, raw fingers found an opening, a rough metallic edge. Rounded sides, a flat middle—

he had stumbled on David Ray Allen's gas-tank submarine, the one they had floated in the summer flood.

Feverishly Garrett dug the tank out of its corn-stubble mooring and emptied it as best he could. He hoped that it had not separated at the seam, or collected a lot of dirt in the bottom. It had to float. Half pushing, half carrying, he dragged it back through the trees toward the Stones. "Hang on, Linnie," he said under his breath. "I'm coming to get you."

Garrett splashed into the water and launched the tank, crawling astride as if it were a horse. His legs hung over at an uncomfortable angle; the cold water numbed them. For a moment he thought that he would sink into the mud and never get out. How would David Ray get the thing going? he wondered. Finally he saw that he could use branches and bushes for hand-holds, pulling himself along. He held his breath and drew himself into the deep water on the downstream side of the Stones, then let himself go. The tank was unsteady, but it was afloat.

A slow sense of wonder made his aching body seem almost warm. Hey, he thought, I'm doing it. Maybe it's going to work. He meant to grab the first long branch that floated by to use as a guide, but he missed and the effort nearly sent him headfirst. Slowly the odd craft righted itself, without toppling Garrett. From bush to tree to rock he went, hand over hand, with the bottom of Granpop's coat trailing in the water and the Stones themselves shielding him from the current. As he neared the ledge he could feel the tug of the main stream, and he could hear Jack Tramp soothing Linnie in his ugly, beautiful voice.

"Heh!" cried Jack Tramp. "Look comin'! See that ship? See that ship comin'?"

The level of the creek had reached the ledge; Garrett's tank crunched against the corner of the nearest stone. He steadied it as best he could with one foot and one hand.

"Come on, Linnie," Garrett coaxed. "Come on and take a ride."

"No. What if I fall in the water?" It was her stubborn voice.

"You won't fall in." Garrett's teeth were chattering, from the cold, he thought. "There's lots of things to hold on to. It's David Ray's tank, Linnie. Don't you want a ride on David Ray's tank?"

"Go on," said Jack Tramp, nudging her toward her brother. "You stay up here, you get all wet. Go on, now." He scooted her toward Garrett, held her coat collar while she made her way, whimpering, from the ledge to the tank. She settled facing Garrett, clinging to his knees.

"It makes my feet all wet," she cried. "It makes me cold."

"Your feet were wet already," Garrett told her sharply. "Now sit still."

Suddenly she wailed. "Where's Mabel? Don't leave Mabel!"

The old man handed her the doll. "I'll come back for you," Garrett promised, looking up at Jack Tramp. The tank bobbled in the water.

"Uh!" Jack coughed. "No need, boy. Water won't come much higher, see? Gets this high—" he pointed just above his waist—"it's got to spread out up in the field." He leaned over and thumped the tank with his finger. "Wouldn't want on that thing, anyway. Sink, with me on it, just like that!" He smacked his palms together, then pushed himself back against the high wall at the end of the Stones. "Get away, now," he said. "Get away. In the morning all this

water, it'll be gone. Me, I'll climb down the way I come up. Be on my way then."

Garrett hesitated, holding the tank as still as he could. He supposed that the old man was right about the level of the water; it couldn't climb the Stones until it had filled the valley, and it would take an ocean of water to do that. Jack wouldn't drown. And he was probably right about the tank, too. It wouldn't hold him. It hadn't floated with Clarence, Garrett remembered. Yet how could he just go away and leave Jack Tramp shivering and coughing with the water and the darkness all around him? He owed the old man something; he owed him a lot. Garrett unbuttoned his huge coat, which still had a few dry spots inside, and carefully took it off. He tossed it toward the center of the ledge.

"Here, Mr. Schilling," he said. "I don't need this—it makes us too heavy." There were other things that he felt he ought to say, but the words didn't come. And anyway, Linnie had started to fuss.

"Go on!" shouted Jack Tramp. He fumbled with the coat, hurrying to get his arms inside the sleeves. "Get away!"

"I'll have someone come get you as soon as I can, honest I will," Garrett said, and he pushed gently away from the side of the Stones.

"Hang on now," he told Linnie. "It's not very far. When we get past the oak tree then we have to go around that bush, and then a little way beyond the picnic stone." He kept talking, kept telling himself. "It isn't even very deep some places, just where the gullies are." He was afraid, but it wasn't stopping him. He knew how the water was: how it smelled, how it felt, how it could fill you up so there wasn't any room for air. He was afraid, but he went right on. Maybe that was the way David Ray felt climbing the Stones, he thought, or even his father—

"Sit still, Linnie!" The tank jiggled dangerously and he had to fight to steady it. Linnie shivered and tried to scoot closer to him. The tank began to roll, and he couldn't stop it. Linnie hit the water before she had time to scream, and Garrett fell beside her. He spluttered, grabbed for a bush. It was Linnie's arm he caught instead, and he yanked hard, pulled her upright. It was too easy, too simple. And then he realized that his feet were in the mud, that he was standing, walking. The deep water was already behind them.

"Hey, come on!" he cried, still pulling at Linnie's arm. She was coughing up her quick swallow of creek water, scrambling for a footing of her own. Her hat, still firmly tied around her neck, floated behind her head, snagging on every branch. Garrett pulled the knotted strings up over her face and let the hat go free.

"We're okay," he told her. Two more steps, and the water was only ankle high. "We're all right," he said, hardly able to believe it himself. "Everything's going to be all right. Just everything. You didn't hear about it yet, Linnie—I forgot. But they found Dad."

Linnie's teeth made a clattering noise, but she said nothing.

"I mean, he's alive and everything." He waited for her to squeal with delight, but she didn't.

"Is he home?"

"Of course he's not home, silly. The war isn't over yet. He's still in France or somewhere."

"I don't know where that is."

"It's a long way from here," he told her. He began to

notice how cold he was, how tired. Linnie clung to his hand in the darkness, and they bumped each other on almost every step.

Linnie stopped without warning and sucked in her breath.

"What's the matter?" Garrett demanded, facing her, trying to see. "Did you hurt your foot or something?"

She began to cry.

"Where?" he asked frantically. "Show me what's wrong —where does it hurt?"

"Mabel's gone!" she wailed. "Mabel got drownded!"

Something inside Garrett exploded. "You and that doll!" he shouted. "You and that crazy worthless rag! You care more about it than you do about Dad, that's what. If you hadn't run off with your precious Stuffed Mabel, we wouldn't be all soaked the way we are now, just about ready to catch pneumonia or something. And neither would poor old Jack Tramp—" His own teeth began to chatter, and he was suddenly ashamed. Linnie wouldn't have run off if he hadn't said she lied. But that had been at noon, and the noontime was a hundred years ago, almost beyond memory. "Never mind," he said. "I'm sorry." He let her lean against him for a minute, crying into his wet shirt.

"We'll go back and look for Mabel when it's dry, okay?" he promised. They'd never find the thing, he thought. But Linnie didn't have to know that now. "We have to get where it's warm," he said to her. "We have to go home. We ought to run, Linnie—can you run?"

She shook her head.

"Try." He dragged her along without waiting for her to agree, through the last of the trees into the dark, wet field. He could scarcely run, himself. He was tired, cold, emptied of feeling, as if all his warmth and energy, every-thing, had dissolved into the flood.

"Garrett!" Linnie cried, pulling him back, snuffling her nose. "Garrett, look! Lightning bugs!"

He glanced up the slope and saw them, all the lanterns and flashlights bobbing toward them, winking with light like giant fireflies.

"Hey!" shouted Garrett. His voice croaked. "Hey, Granpop! Everybody! Here we are!"

CHAPTER 14

Afterward, Garrett couldn't remember what came next. Over and over, in the strange, familiar country of fever, he sloshed through the dark water around the Stones—sometimes with his father, sometimes with David Ray, sometimes with Clarence. Once he talked to an old man sitting in a rocking chair with a pumpkin on his lap, singing to it.

"Drink this! Swallow!" That was Aunt Em.

"Good enough. Doing all right." That was the doctor from Springtown.

His mother ought to go to work, he kept thinking. She'd be late. She sat close to him and he fixed his eyes on her hands, with the fingers knotted like bows. Once he heard her say, "Wait till Andy hears about it," and that made him smile. Or he thought he must be smiling. There was a question he wanted to ask, but he couldn't remember it. Whenever he tried to talk the words turned stubborn and hid behind the ache in his head.

Then all at once, or so it seemed to him, Garrett woke out of a dreamless sleep and found himself on the living room couch under two blankets and a quilt. His legs were entirely numb. I'm hurt, he thought with wonder: paralyzed. Maybe I had polio like President Roosevelt, and I'll have to ride around in a wheelchair all the rest of my life. Horrified, he raised his head to see what damage had been done to his body. What he saw was Linnie, sitting on his feet. She wore flannel pajamas, a sweater, and one of Aunt Em's aprons tied twice around her middle.

"For pete's sake, would you move?" As soon as she shifted her weight, the feeling crept back into his toes.

"I'm all better," she said with importance, "but you're not. I'm reading you a story." She held a magazine, flipping pages at random.

"Pretending to, you mean." He sat up carefully to keep the room from wobbling.

"I am too reading," Linnie insisted. "I'm a nurse and I'm taking care of you."

"Nurses don't read you stories," he said.

"Well, they should." Her lip rolled forward in a pout.

Everything was the same, Garrett thought. The wallpaper hadn't changed color, the furniture was all in place, Linnie was still contrary. He parted the curtains behind the couch, looked out and blinked at the hazy autumn sunshine. Beyond the bare maples was the road, and beyond that a glimpse of the lane. Something clicked inside the boy's head, and he remembered what it was that he wanted to know.

It was Granpop, finally, who explained everything, telling it slowly to make sure that he understood. Mr. Grant had got Jack Tramp off the ledge at the Stones using a rope and an inner tube borrowed from Fiddler's Garage. *Clarence's father!* thought Garrett with disbelief. Then the men had put Jack into Paul Darcy's car and driven him straight to Springtown, to the hospital. Everyone had expected him to die. He was suffering from a long list of disorders that should have been attended to long before, the doctor had told them, including bad lungs. "Too many cigars," Aunt Em put in firmly. "I always knew it."

"By rights," said Granpop, shaking his head, "if he was an ordinary man, he'd be dead. They figure he had a heart attack, or next thing to it, up on that ledge. Looks like he's going to make it, though."

"Is he coming home, then?" Garrett wanted to know.

"It's not likely, ever," said Aunt Em. "He won't be able to do for himself for a long time. When he's through with the hospital he'll have to go to the County Farm."

Garrett blinked. "Does he know that?"

"It's hard to tell," Granpop said. "Sometimes when I go in to see him he's sittin' up and carryin' on just like always. Wants to know if we're lookin' after his house and all, and are you kids better, and when can he get out of there. Other times he doesn't even know who I am."

The boy stared at the ceiling. He tried to picture Jack with nurses fussing over him, all tidied up and a white sheet under his chin. He'd be hating that, Garrett was sure.

"It doesn't seem right," he said. "Poor old Jack Tramp."

"Mr. Schilling, you mean." Granpop smiled a crooked smile. "That's what they call him up at the hospital and half the time he doesn't answer—hardly knows who they're talking to."

"Where did he get that name 'Jack Tramp,' anyway?" Garrett asked.

"Goes clear back to the last war, that does," Aunt Em said. "You remember, Leo? When folks pestered him about his name he'd say, 'Just call me Jack.' "

Garrett's history book began with the Revolution, and his teacher thought the Civil War was so interesting that her class never seemed to get any farther than 1870. Garrett didn't know anything about World War I. "What do you mean?" he asked Aunt Em. "What was the matter with his name?"

"It was German-sounding, child. The country was at war with Germany then, too. People went wild, crazy-like. Anything German, they hated. The City Council in Springtown even changed the names of some of the streets that had been named after German settlers."

Granpop sighed. "It's not so bad this time," he said. "Folks seem to have better sense about who we're fighting and who we're not."

"Yeah," said Garrett, lying back against the arm of the couch. "I guess so." He hoped none of the boys ever mentioned the war game again; he wanted to forget it.

There came a day, finally, when Garrett got himself dressed and stayed up all day, and then Aunt Em said he could have company. About time, too, he thought. He had read every comic book and magazine in the house two or three times and had listened to the radio so much that one of its tubes had burned out. That afternoon, in answer to his unspoken wish, David Ray appeared at the back door. He was a messenger from school, he said, with one hand full of homework and the other full of get-well messages designed by Garrett's classmates. Most of the cards were decorated with American flags and tanks and aircraft carriers, except for Gracie Dean's, which showed a bunch of flowers colored with purple crayon.

"Ugh," said David when they looked at that one, and rolled his eyes to make Garrett laugh.

"Don't you get rowdy in there!" called Aunt Em from the kitchen.

David Ray made a face and settled himself comfortably on the end of the couch. "You know what I would have done if it had been me?" he began. "I'd have climbed the Stones from this side, see, clear up over the top, and gone *down* to the ledge and got her back that way."

"Like fun," Garrett said. "You couldn't have got her back up to the top from that ledge. It's just about straight up." Usually when David Ray talked about what he would do, Garrett worried in silence, wondering if he could ever do the same. Now he didn't care.

David Ray whistled softly. "I still can't believe it," he said. "You—on that tank. And the old Nazi out there with you in the dark. That's creepy." He whistled again. "What was it like, huh? What did he do? Did he yell at you and everything?"

Garrett chewed his lip. "Well, he sang—sort of. To Linnie."

"Sang!" David Ray's lively face was still with disbelief. "No kidding!"

"I swear." Garrett traced the scroll design of the slip-cover fabric with one finger, not looking at the other boy. "He's an okay sort of guy, you know it? When he gets to the County Farm I'm going to have Granpop take me out to see him."

"Are you crazy?" David Ray stared at him. "That place stinks. Don't you remember last year when we went out from school to sing Christmas carols? We thought all the plaster was coming right down on our heads from that old cracked ceiling, don't you remember? And how about that old lady who chewed tobacco and drooled all over Gracie's skirt? How about that?"

Garrett shrugged.

"Anyway," continued David Ray, "old what's-his-name is a Nazi, for cripe's sake!"

"He is not!" The heat in Garrett's face felt like fever. "We made that up and you know it. What's the matter with having a name like Schilling? It's just a name, isn't it? It doesn't make him an enemy, does it?"

David Ray leaned backward, holding up his hands for protection. "Hey, I dunno. Okay? Don't get huffy." He leaned farther, draping himself upside down over the arm of the couch, so that he was nearly standing on his head. "Clarence told us about the pumpkin thing," he said, "but he hasn't told his old man yet. He's working up to it."

Garrett sighed. "You're getting sort of purple," he said. "Maybe you'd better stand up."

Aunt Em came in with a pill for Garrett to take—he still had to take them every four hours exactly—and she told David it was time for him to go home. Or if he didn't have to go just yet, he could come to the kitchen and do something to amuse Linnie, who was every bit as bored as Garrett had been. Given the choice, David Ray went home.

"Don't you mope around now," Aunt Em said to Garrett. "There's a surprise for supper. One for you and one for Linnie." A special dessert, he guessed. Rice pudding for him and custard for Linnie. Or maybe apple dumplings with their initials on top.

But Linnie's surprise could not be eaten. Beside her plate

she found Stuffed Mabel, scrubbed and mended. A bit flatter than before and somewhat faded, but without a doubt Stuffed Mabel. For Garrett there was a letter from his father.

After so many days and nights on the couch, his own bed felt like a homecoming. Bedsprings squeaked in the room next door, his mother yawned, Linnie coughed a little. Everything was familiar and comfortable and good.

Silently Garrett reached for the picture on the night-stand and drew it under his blanket. How is it with you? he demanded, without words, of his father. What's it like? His father was wounded in the shoulder, but he hadn't said how bad it was. He had been all alone in a bombed-out shed on an abandoned farm, not knowing how to get back to his own men, not knowing where the enemy was. When the old farmer's wife had finally ventured home to look for food, she had found him and nursed him and helped him find his way. What was it like? He ached to know every detail; somehow, the not knowing separated him from his father more than distance.

The boy touched all four corners of the picture frame as if it were a lucky charm, and squeezed his eyes tight. His father would come home grinning, just the same as ever. His father would come home and do the chores for Granpop and make Aunt Em laugh till she cried and hug Mom until *she* cried and they'd all be on a picnic that would last forever.

Garrett sat up and held the photograph under the window, where it caught a faint glimmer of light. He pressed his nose right down on the familiar likeness, trying to see

it, trying to be sure of the one crooked eyebrow. There was nothing different about the picture, he was certain. Yet in that deep and hidden part of his mind where he kept secrets from himself, Garrett was just as certain that something, somehow, had changed.

And besides that, Linnie was crying.

"Hey," he whispered. "What's the matter?"

"She's too hard." Stuffed Mabel, swung by one foot, came thumping out from under the covers. "She's got lumps now." Linnie sniffled.

"I know, Linnie, but just think what she's been through —all that dirty water and mud and sticker bushes. You know what Mom said about finding her under a log, all doubled up."

Linnie blew her nose. "I know." She had pulled the covers up over her head so that he could scarcely hear her. "Everybody told me that." She coughed, and her brother knew without seeing that her cheeks were getting red as two roses. "Garrett?"

"What?"

"She just won't ever be the same, will she?"

In the dark he shook his head. "I guess not," he said, holding the photograph tight to his chest. He knew the thing that he had not wanted to know: his father wouldn't be the same either. Nothing was, really. He wasn't the same himself. He peered out into the night where Jack Tramp's lonely roof gleamed in the starshine. Everything was different—some things better, some things worse. And his father wasn't going to come home like some long-ago wizard and smile everything back into place the way it used to be. There was no sense expecting it.

"Garrett?"

"What?"

"I don't really care if Mabel isn't as soft as she was before. I still want her." The rag doll flopped obligingly at Linnie's tug and disappeared under the covers.

"Sure," he said. "I know how you feel." Carefully he put their father's picture back on the nightstand. "Good night, Linnie. Good night, Dad. Come home soon," he said. Right out loud.